OCTOPUS SUMMER

OCTOPUS SUMMER

W. MALCOLM DORSON

a novel

SOFT SKULL

AN IMPRINT OF COUNTERPOINT

BERKELEY

Library of Congress Cataloging-in-Publication Data
Dorson, W. Malcolm.
Octopus Summer : A Novel / W. Malcolm Dorson.
pages cm
1. Young men—Fiction. 2. Upper class—New York (State)—Long Island. 3. Summer employment—Fiction. 4. Friendship—Fiction. I. Title.
PS3604.O775O38 2014
813'.6—dc23
2013044835

ISBN 978-1-61902-298-0

Cover design by Sophia Newbold
Interior Design by Tabitha Lahr

Soft Skull Press
An Imprint of COUNTERPOINT
1919 Fifth Street
Berkeley, CA 94710
www.softskull.com

Printed in the United States of America
Distributed by Publishers Group West

10 9 8 7 6 5 4 3 2 1

For Grandmaman

OCTOPUS SUMMER

PROLOGUE

I TROT ACROSS THE BRIDAL path, up the steps to the reservoir, and lay eyes on the still meadow of glass. A soft mist rises above reflections of the City. Heavy silence. Too serene. High-rises tower over trees in the distance. All around people work, fight, love, create, destroy, and die, but I am transient. I am young. I rush through my stretches and begin a soft jog north. The path is clear and empty, apart from remnants of last night's rain. No job, no school, no family, no friends, no responsibility, no concern. Nobody to cheer me on. Nobody to hinder me. I try and look back at the skyline, but it's difficult to run with your head wound back. I zigzag and develop a stitch. I look ahead and perfect my form. I stare six feet in front of me. Not too far ahead. Definitely not behind. Not anymore. I focus on what's next. The inevitable. Follow the path laid out for me, around the track and back to where I began. I set my breathing pattern. One long inhale through my nose. Two quick exhales through my mouth. My seventh-grade soccer coach told me this will sooth my mind and get more oxygen to my muscles. I don't feel like I'm getting enough oxygen to my brain, but I go with it. In, out, out. In, out, out. I stick out my chest. I look good. High knees, long strides. I tire quickly and begin to dodge puddles and leap over model rivers and lakes. Splash. I'm humbled. The ponds grow larger and sandy riverbeds turn to mud. The path is empty and I can navigate through the narrow dry sand bridges, but I prefer the pleasure paths through the grass. Never too far from the track though. Always back on in between puddles. I run at a quicker gait than I had imagined and am almost to the end. No more sidetracks. My face is flushed and my breathing is off. "Finish up strong," a Mather Academy motto. Running straight, now sprinting forward as fast as I can. Fuck the puddles. I go right through each pile of sludge like sequential finish lines. No regard to the dirty consequences, I just want to finish and immerse myself back into the City.

PART 1

1

BRENDA

"CALLUM LITTLEFIELD, table for two."

It was a stifling July night in Manhattan, and I was ready for sex. Brenda and I agreed to meet at Rouge 66, a trendy bistro my sister had told me about. The waiters wore blue pants and women's V-neck T-shirts. The music was European techno and belonged in the elevator of a Chelsea hotel. A booth of older women checked me out. Brief eye contact—not really wanting to know if they were friends of my mother's or Upper East Side cougars. Too much risk for the former. Not enough potential with the latter. I unbuttoned the second button of my shirt and rolled up my sleeves. Too much? I buttoned the shirt back up. Mood lights obnoxiously changed from a pale pink to blue. It was the type of place I hated, but I knew that Brenda would love it. I was on to my second vodka soda by the time she arrived. My mother's drink, splash of soda. Then another to wash down her Xanax. Brenda looked like a lost child as she walked through the door. Not knowing my last name, I watched her fumble with the maître d' before waving her over. I noticed she was a couple of inches taller than me as I pulled her chair out for her. She was overdressed for the place with a tight black backless cocktail number, but I didn't care. Better overdressed than under. I didn't love the fact that she had four more rings on her left ear than on her right and that she wore a gothic choker, but whatever, she looked sexy as hell and my parents were away. This was my night. It was finally going to happen.

"Sorry I'm late," said Brenda. "The subway took for*ever*."

"Oh, no worries. I just got here myself."

The first five minutes of dinner could have been thirty. Brenda and I had nothing in common, so I just kept topping off her glass and searching for small talk.

"I like your chain," I said, motioning to the sterling silver around her neck. I hated it. It was like something from a nail salon in Spanish Harlem.

"Thanks, I got it for my confirmation." She pulled out a cross from between her small, firm breasts. "I mean, I'm not religious or anything. Total atheist. Had to do it for my parents back in the day. I just keep this cause I think it looks nice or whatever."

"Would you like an oyster?" I asked, smothering one in cocktail sauce and lemon.

"I'm a vegetarian."

By the time I finished my steak tartare, we were both a little sloppy. Brenda rambled on about her senior art project, something about creating a series of prints combining Asian patterns and city landscapes. I smiled, nodded, and drifted.

". . . so yeah, the rich can send their kids to school, and the poor can get these scholarships, but what are the normal fifty- to sixty-thousand-dollar-a-year-household-income families supposed to do if their kids aren't genius scholarship winners? They probably work harder than the fuckin' rich and the welfare crowd combined, ya know? It's bullshit!"

I snapped back into her lecture. How did we get here? Where was I? I was polite and tried to pay attention, focusing on her waxed eyebrows to feign eye contact. I was trying, but it didn't seem like this was going anywhere. When her elbows graced the table and her hiccups became even more audible, I unbuttoned my shirt again. This night was over.

"Totally." I nodded. "I mean, it's shitty for everyone, but the worst part is that these guys are more focused on winning their next campaign than on tackling anything legit when in office."

She paused and looked at me with a dull, blank stare. "Hiccup."

Was that a dumb comment? Was she going to throw up? Where's the doggy bag?

Then, suddenly, her bare foot slid up the cuff of my pants and moved up and down my argyle sock. "Hmmm. I didn't expect that out of you," she purred.

I thought about making a move, but it still took me one more cocktail to work up the courage.

"Hey, if you don't have plans after this, would you want to come back to my place for another drink?" I asked nervously. She had turned the tables and suddenly had much more control of the evening than I did.

"Yes," she said with a devilish smile.

I paid the bill, and we headed uptown in an airconditionless cab. My slacks stuck to the melting pleather of the seats, and I could see tiny beads of sweat glimmer on Brenda's forehead. The air smelled of old curry and mint air freshener. Was I wearing deodorant? I couldn't remember. We kissed a little and talked even less. I opened the window. The wind messed up my hair, and I closed it again. By the time we pulled up to my house, I was sweating while my hands shivered. I had never been with a girl like this before. She was a tomcat.

I poured two stiff screwdrivers and led her out to the garden before running to the bathroom and rubbing on some Old Spice. Brenda walked slowly gazing up at the ceilings. She eventually broke the ice.

"Hey, if your parents aren't home, I have some bud," she said.

I hadn't smoked pot since school, but I was pretty drunk and didn't want to turn her down.

"My parents are not even in the country. That would be great."

She laughed at me as I coughed up a lung after my first hit.

"Sorry, I've been running a lot lately. Think that went down the wrong pipe." By the time Brenda packed the third bowl, I couldn't stop laughing.

"What's this nug called?"

"Mauie Wowie. Do you like it?"

"Yeah, hah, it's awesome. What are you doing this weekend?"

"Not sure yet. I'm around. How about you?"

"Nothing. Tell me about your parents."

"Hah. Seriously? Calm down there. Are you going to give me the tour or what?"

Putty in her hands. It's funny how easy it is to fall in love after a few drinks.

On our way upstairs, we stopped in my dad's office for a detour make-out session on the couch. I thought this would be cool and that the room would impress her, but she would not stop talking about how much she liked the antique demons on the mantel. I wished my father would throw those out.

"Let's go upstairs." I pulled on one of her leather bracelets and marched her up the steps. This was it. I focused on each step before me.

When we got to my room, there was no more talking. She pushed me down on the bed and went straight for my slacks. What was going on? I had never had a girl take control like this. I loved it but didn't want to seem like a pussy, so I pushed her up and pulled off her dress before rolling her over. She wasn't wearing a bra. I leaned in for a kiss. When I pushed myself back up, I looked down at Brenda. She was lying motionless like a dead fish waiting for my next move. I froze. What happened? I didn't really know what to do, so I started thrusting my hips into her. My boxers were on, and as I look back on it, this couldn't have been very comfortable for her. This went on for a little, and she began to breathe deeper. She must have been faking it, and I decided it would be a good idea for me to do the same. She flipped on top of me, and I kept rubbing into her, over and over. We both began to sweat. Her crucifix dangled off her breasts, and Jesus danced on my chest. I lost control of my breathing, and she continued to have her way with me.

Brenda then fell back on top of me and breathed into my ear as she kissed my neck. I tried kissing her back but got some of her hair in my mouth so just focused on massaging her back.

"That feels so good." She whispered into my ear and then nibbled on its lobe. "Do you have a condom?" YES! This was it! Magic words. I was in. I leaned over to my bedside table, pulled open the drawer, and took out a Trojan.

"Here we go. Just a sec," I said as I ripped open the packet.

"Hah, wait a second tiger . . . What are you doing?"

"Um didn't you just ask me if I had a condom?"

"Um, I said I should probably get going. It's getting kind of late . . ." My face went numb. I was *such* an idiot. Brenda must have picked up on my embarrassment because she smiled and started kissing me again.

I think she was willing of course and probably wanted to make the next move, but I didn't sleep with Brenda that night. She did go down on me, but there was no sex. Well, real sex. Actually, I put her in a taxi about ten minutes later. Don't get me wrong. Like I told you, I got my kicks and all. But I didn't lose my virginity that night.

2

HOME ALONE

HUNGOVER AS HELL, I felt like someone had stuck a small axe into my forehead. A strong current pulsed around my brain, pushing my eyeballs against every nerve in the region. My neck had trouble carrying the weight of my skull to the bathroom, so I leaned over and let my head hang under a cold faucet. I hacked up a brown oyster of phlegm and began to feel a little better. Today was a new day. I was eighteen years old, alone in New York, and had the time and means to do as I pleased. I was away from Miralva, away from the Octopus, and back in my zone. It was a crisp, sunny day, and as I looked out the window, I developed an overwhelming feeling that the summer was mine.

After an American cheese omelet, I thought running the reservoir would help dampen the headache. Bad idea. I had always thought of myself as an excellent runner, but I could barely make it halfway around the track. I tried using the spandex wrapped, heart-shaped bottom of the woman ahead of me as inspiration, but that only worked for so long. It was pretty embarrassing having a thirty-something-year-old woman and then a middle-aged man and then a fifteen-year-old boy pass me, so I developed a fake limp and walked the rest of the track. As I reached the end, I saw the ninety-year-old man who runs around the reservoir at least five times a day with his two gold medals flashing around his neck. The reservoir's mascot. This old guy could run five loops a day, and I barely made it once at a walk. I picked up my pace and jogged the rest of the way, forcing a smile as I ran past him. I finally approached the Guggenheim and slowed back to a mother's power walk. At least I made the effort.

I kept trying to run the reservoir for the following week until I could finally complete the circle. I aimlessly wandered the Met, the Guggenheim, and the Frick. I slept a lot, and I even went to a movie by myself, which was sad and lonely as hell. I tried meeting up with friends, but they still seemed pissed about the whole situation back at school. My writing classes gave me consistency, but besides that, I was a wanderer. I called my grandmother daily, explaining that I was far too busy with homework to come out for the next few weeks. I could tell that she was hurt, but I could not sleep in that house. Not with Miralva there.

A few days later, I noticed an invitation to the Wildlife Conservation Society party posted on the bulletin board in our kitchen. A picture of a swan-like bird graced the background of the invitation, with committee and junior committee member names in the foreground. It was sent from the Carsons. Thursday, July 10, only a week away. I guessed that Astrid, my mother's goddaughter, needed an extra boy at her table. At first I cringed at the idea of making small talk with family friends all night, but the more I thought about it, the more I realized that many of my old "friends" would probably be there and that it would probably be a terrific party with tons of cute prospects. I didn't have anything else to do anyway. "Dress: Safari Chic." Girls in animal prints? Couldn't complain. It was at the Central Park Zoo, and that alone would make for a pretty cool scene. I replied to Mrs. Carson that I would love to go and made plans to grab a drink with my old camp buddy, Collin Patterson, at Bemelmans Bar beforehand. Patterson should have gone to Mather with me to play squash but he ended up at Groton so he could play lacrosse as well.

Collin was a great kid, but his parents were coming out of a long messy divorce, and he wasn't taking it well. Mr. Patterson worked in the World Trade Center, and when his wife saw the terror of the 9/11 strikes on television, she immediately called his cell phone to see if he was all right. When the dumb-ass picked up, he said that everything was fine at the office (forty-fifth floor of Tower One). "Busy day honey, gotta run," was his notorious quote. Apparently he was on the fourteenth floor of the Waldorf with his secretary and completely oblivious to the whole situation. Poor Collin.

Anyway, the party had the makings of a fun evening, and I finally had something to look forward to.

3

BEMELMANS

I SPENT THE DAY OF the benefit drinking Newman's pink lemonade vodka cocktails on the roof of our townhouse. The scorching black tar surface stained my Vilebrequin bathing suit, but I did not mind as long as my face was getting some color. My low tolerance and fair complexion got the best of me, and by the time I went downstairs to prepare, I was roller coaster dizzy, and my cheeks felt like a freshly spanked bottom. I took a long, cold shower.

I remembered my last black-tie dinner dance. It was the Infirmary or maybe the Junior Assembly Ball in the City this past winter and ended with me welcoming some poor girl to society on her knees in our basement. A knighting ceremony, if you will.

After showering, shaving my peach fuzz, combing my hair, shining my shoes, putting on my tux—I mean black tie. "Tuxes are for weddings in Hicksville," my father always said—I spent twenty minutes perfecting the imperfection of my bowtie and the three points of my handkerchief. I was ready to go. Keys: check. Phone: check. Wallet: check—fuck! My ID. I had been so wrapped up in my struggles this summer that I had completely forgotten to get another ID. Restaurants were one thing, but bars were another animal all together. Too late now. I'd drink table wine at dinner and figure something else out later.

Knowing that half of the guys there would be coming in from Greenwich and wearing their matching Lilly or Vineyard Vines cummerbund and bowtie sets in pathetic attempts to rebel against the norm, I decided to stick with the traditional black. It was my way of rebelling against the rebels, if that makes any sense at all.

It was six o'clock and I was supposed to meet Patterson at seven. I had spent the last couple of days so desperately trying to entertain myself that I had actually become pretty excited about this little shindig. I had a few pretzels and poured myself three fingers of Dewar's, as I had seen my father do before parties.

I could barely stand the Scotch's scent, so I ran downstairs and cleaned my palate with a Mint Milano in the kitchen.

I killed the rest of the time watching two episodes of *Family Matters* in my father's office. My parents used to let me watch two TV shows a night after school, and I always chose ones about black families. I thought they were hysterical. My parents thought I was retarded. I sat up straight in my father's desk chair so that I would not wrinkle my pants. Urkel wasn't as funny as I remembered.

The lights on Park Avenue were already fading, as people had begun retreating to their summer homes for the season. I was about to hop in a taxi but noticed the traffic and could not help smirking at the standstill of bridge-and-tunnel visitors. Con

Edison had set up a construction tent a few blocks down and blocked two lanes heading downtown. Dozens of cars filled with hairspray and testosterone inched into the City for Thursday nights of gold chains, tight shirts, and bizarre sideburns. Guess everybody really had the same intentions: Get fucked up to the point where you put down your guard and feel comfortable trying to get laid. We all just had different settings for the procedure. I imagined the guys blasting techno dance beats from their Pontiac were looking forward to cheap blow and thumping Top 40 at McWhatever on Murray Hill.

I was ready for a night of small talk and large drinks. I hadn't really been in touch with any of my "friends" since getting kicked out of Mather in May, and I was looking forward to some company. I still couldn't believe that I didn't graduate with my class. Everything had been ripped out from under me. Whatever. It would be nice to meet new people. It had been two months since Michelle and I had broken up, and I was ready to move on. I made a right on 88th and walked briskly down Madison Avenue. As I walked past William Sonoma, someone opened the door, and a gust of air conditioning sent a pleasant chill across my sunburnt cheeks. I was thankful it wasn't strong enough to push my hair out of place. I purposely dragged my feet a little to scratch the bottom of my loafers, which had recently been resoled and felt too slippery. While pausing outside of a gourmet catering store to check my reflection in the window, I saw a limo filled with loud, drunk teenagers in black tie fly by behind me. One was leaning outside the window with a joint in his hand, singing along to Journey's "Don't Stop Believin'" from the stereo. Idiots. I began having second thoughts about the party.

I just didn't love dealing with some specific crowds, "Gree-noix," pushy Upper Eastsiders, etc. I know, I know. Who was I to talk? But still. It got fierce sometimes. "OTT," over the top as my mother would say. She had perfected the art of discreet arrogance. All the same, they *were* all just a little over the top for me, and way too in your face about it. I meant the types who killed the idea that WASPs were generally thrifty. The ones with designer jewelry and garages filled with flashy SUV Porsches, Lexuses, Mercedeses, and BMWs. I just needed a drink with Patterson.

The doorman at the Carlyle gave me a warm smile and showed me to the bar. I hadn't been there since I was about seven for tea with my mother and sister, but I immediately loved the place. The room smelled of oak and the waiters looked like friendly Irish grandfathers. Businessmen in English suits took the edge off with fine Scotches and talked about themselves and their friends with fervent interest. Upper-crust tourists filled in the blanks. A Bobby Short reincarnate sat at the piano and graced the room with the smooth sound of Sinatra's "My Way." Bemelmans was a classic. I remember my Mom telling me it was named after Ludwig Bemelmans, the illustrator of the Madeline books, which were always my older sister Julia's favorites. It had quirky New York cartoon scenery all over the walls, the old New York. Legend has it that he painted the bar in return for a lifelong room at the Carlyle and an open tab at the bar. Not a bad deal for a cartoonist.

Patterson had a fine people-watching table and a beer waiting for me. Not too aggressive, but I guess I appreciated his pace.

"Hey bro, how's it going? I heard about Mather and everything. Sorry to hear it, man. You holding up alright?" It didn't take long for the Upper East Side to hear that I'd been kicked out of boarding school for selling drugs.

"I'm fine, man. Have actually been having a pretty interesting little summer. I was out in Long Island for a while, but my 'rents left the country and am now back at my place . . . solo."

"Oh shit! Open house?! That's sick, dude."

"Hah, no, man. No parties. You know my dad, but it's nice to have some privacy. I met this chick at a writing class I'm taking at NYU and brought back her home on day one. Not a big deal . . ."

"No way?! You take her down?"

"Yah dude." Patterson gave me a fist touch across the table.

"So this party should be stacked, huh?! I'm thinking perfect storm of city, boarding school, and college chicks," Patterson speculated.

"Yeah, man, should be a ton of faces. I'm not positive I'm going to go, though."

"What the fuck? How come? You're dressed. No way you're leaving me on this. Don't be a pussy."

"I don't know, dude. I just can't really deal with the crowd anymore. It's too much of the same crap."

He pretended he knew what I was talking about.

"Yeah, it's bullshit." I'm pretty sure he thought I was off my rocker.

"You should come, though. Fuck Mather kids. There will be a bunch of other people."

"Yeah, but I also got my ID taken in that whole ordeal as well. I don't know how tough they are going to be at this party."

"Not a problem, my man." Patterson pulled out a fake California driver's license from a bodega on West 4th Street. "I always carry a backup. Consider it yours. Now let's get you another cocktail." Patterson ordered two vodka sodas for us.

"Thanks man. I know. You're right. You're right. You're right." I got over it. The ID could work. We looked pretty similar, and bartenders barely ever look at pictures. I was ready. It's all a game, roar with laughter to the dullest of jokes, widen eyes at uninteresting facts about schools or summer plans, and tear up at every sob story of a broken relationship, sick pet, or tacky neighbor. We paid our bill and made off to the party. Go time.

4

ZOO PARTY

I HAD NEVER SEEN the Central Park Zoo at night before. It looked haunted from the outside as streetlights illuminated the old brick arsenal draped in ivy. We made our way around the building and saw the animal kingdom lit up. The outdoor seal tank had white Christmas lights all over it, a woman walked around the dining tent carrying a boa constrictor on her shoulders, and I saw various long-stemmed birds walking around freely in the gardens.

There was a flock of rare, tanned Chapin-ites at the entrance of the tent, so I parted with Patterson and darted directly to the bathroom to straighten up. Ah, the subtle differences between the Upper East Side girls school species.

"Brearley girls become doctors, Spence girls marry doctors, and Chapin girls have affairs with doctors," my mother used to say.

The bathroom was anything but glamorous, as the room was made up of a separate tent with port-o-potties. I chuckled as I saw a group of guys outside one of the toilets making covertly obvious handshake exchanges and wondered if they actually enjoyed blowing cocaine off of toilet seats that had been occupied by sweaty New York construction workers only hours before. I noticed one guy around my age had forgotten to wipe his nose and still had a trace of white powder outlining his nostril. I probably should have told him but opted against the idea. I didn't know him and didn't want to diminish his table's dinner conversation. I made my way to the mirror, fixed my bowtie, straightened my hair, checked my studs, made sure my cummerbund was on the right way (pockets up to catch your crumbs), and prepared myself for hours of schmoozing. Time for preppy zombie mode.

Patterson was stuck in a corner mingling with a few Palm Beach prunes with whom I had no intention of talking, so I gave him a wave and gestured toward the Carsons. As I walked out of the tent and crossed the room toward my hosts, something, or someone, caught my eye. Too petite to be conventionally beautiful, but she was my Helen. My eyes were locked in on this Trojan woman when I knocked right into my hosts. I think I almost tipped Mrs. Carson over, but she was far too stressed to notice. She was pretty involved with the Wildlife Society and had apparently been active in planning this party.

"Where have you been, Callum? We've been looking for you. Have you said hello to Astrid?"

Astrid was right there. She rolled her eyes, and I smiled. Luckily for me, Mrs. Carson dove into her purse for her misplaced Xanax before she could grill me any longer.

"Here are your Tic Tacs, honey," Mr. Carson said as he passed her the tiny white football. After a few apologies and hellos, I was back to the subject at hand.

"Who is that?" I asked Astrid, gesturing to the blonde girl with Julie Andrews eyes.

"Oh, you mean the one in the black-and-white dress?"

"Yeah," I said, trying to sound casual. She was stunning. Even her dress was incredible. White with black dots, it ran down to her ankles in the back but ruffled up a little in the front. It was a little low cut in front and very low cut behind, exposing most of her back. Pretty bold, to be honest, but she pulled it off gracefully. It hung on every curve of her body perfectly.

"Stop!" Astrid slapped me, and I realized that I had spaced out staring at her and that she was staring right back. I snapped my neck back around.

"You were drooling!"

"I know! I'm sorry. I spaced out. Tell me she didn't see." I knew that she had.

"That's Layla Semmering. Do you want me to introduce you? She went to Groton with me. I think she has a boyfriend, though . . ."

"No, no it's okay. I think I've made enough of an impression."

Astrid pet my hair as if I were her little brother, shook her head, and walked away.

Who cared if she had a boyfriend? Even if she did, there was no rock on her finger. I was so mad at myself for being caught staring that I decided to sip away my anxiety. A heap of nineteen-year-old boys and fifty-five-year-old men, with the sporadic alcoholic mother, engulfed the bar. I weaved my way through the broken line, managing to only be spilled on once.

I finally made my way up to the bar and began focusing on eye contact with the bartender.

"Black Label on the rocks," I said to him as he attended

another guest. I needed to play a little catch-up. The bartender smiled and moved on to someone else. Five foot eight, blonde, and a sunburn fit for a ten-year-old is not a good combination when you're trying to get a drink. I repeated my order a little louder and noticed that Layla was right at the other end of the bar. Fuck. Okay, I had to go introduce myself. I stepped back just as the bartender turned his head and gave me a stern look.

"Try again, kid."

A wrench of doubt shot through my stomach. I was stuck. I could not back off of this challenge now, not with Layla in the audience. What killed me about it was that, as he rejected me, he was pouring a screwdriver to Marty Rittenhouse, who was a year below me at Saint Sebastian's. I offered the bartender Patterson's ID with a smile and pretended that I got this all the time.

"Nope, I know that you're not twenty-one, kid. You look twelve. Now order something else or step aside." Ouch. He didn't even look at the license.

I was so pissed off that I didn't even reply. A hot steam of anger rose through my chest when I heard a chuckle and felt a long hand on my shoulder.

"Ouch. Tough luck, Callum." Owen Beekman, a complete prick and my freshman-year dorm-mate from Mather, said with his shit-eating grin. I really hoped Layla wasn't still looking.

"Fuck off, Beekman," I said as I brushed his long, bony fingers off of my jacket. With his tall, skinny frame, Beekman always had a condescending way of looking down on you. He was trying to be an asshole. We used to be friends. We were actually on the same hall our first two years together at Mather, when he still had braces and was afraid to talk to girls, much less have the arrogance to poke fun at me. He was on my notorious list and also lost the privilege to graduate with our class. He had ignored me all summer and obviously still held a grudge. After brushing away my comment, he ordered a vodka tonic, looked down at me again, shook his head, and walked away. Jerk. I checked for Layla, and she was still there smiling. Could this get any worse?

Back to the bartender. I was furious. No chance in hell was I going to be defeated, so I just stood there and stared him down. Who the hell was this middle-aged, balding, overweight, no-class, assclown to not serve *ME* a drink? Look around, ass. Sure I was on the younger side, but LOTS of these kids were still in school and underage! I was about to explode. Layla was going to think I was a complete joke. I had to put this embarrassing bar scene behind me and go introduce myself. I looked for her back in the crowd when suddenly another hand tapped me on my shoulder. This one with long red nails.

"Soooorry, I don't ussuwally dew this honey, but you are just too adooowrable for me to NOT set you up with my daw-da," said the tipsy forty-something-year-old trespasser in a burgundy dress. Her voice was a torturous blend of Queens and New Jersey. I wanted to turn away and find Layla, but I was not ready, and this woman was at least a distraction from my enemy behind the counter. "Pam" chatted my ear off for a solid half-hour. Not that I really minded, though. Schmoozing with adults had always been an effective way to build up my ego, and at that moment, I needed it. Besides, I was totally eating up the idea of Layla wondering what was going on between this mysterious older woman and me. Who am I kidding? She probably hadn't even noticed. After ten minutes of listening, I had had enough of her banter and began to dominate the conversation. I looked over and made brief eye contact with Layla. Yes! Mather, future in college, Long Island, traveling, her daughter, blah blah blah. I was back. I said good-bye and was through with her, feeling like a young "master of the universe" once again. Layla was nowhere in sight.

She had vanished. I walked around from table to table polishing off other people's wounded soldiers until I saw Collin, who was talking to a tiny little firecracker I knew from tennis camp. Her black thong showed through her zebra-print dress. I started to go over to say hello, but I heard the bell signaling that it was time for dinner. Everyone was already seated by the time I reached Mrs. Carson across the room, and I began to feel a little bit like a moron. When I got to the table, Mrs. Carson signaled that the younger generation of the Carson party was at table sixty-eight. She pointed across the stiff, silent room, and I almost died. I was sticking out like a sore thumb. Layla was sure to see me. What a goof. I power walked through the crowded room, hopping over chairs, trying not to trip and throwing out "pardons" and "excuse mes" every five seconds. Halfway to the table, Sinatra's "Come Fly With Me" began, and an Anglo-Saxon Chinese dragon of white dresses started marching toward me. The ladies of the Junior Committee, all dressed in white like the swans they were saving, shuffled toward the podium at the front of the tent. A porky little blonde who was probably twenty-eight and too old for this type of thing led the way. She paused as she saw me in her path, and the sheep behind her piled on like a nightmare on I-95. I waved, put my head down, and darted out of the way.

After much embarrassment, I finally made it to the table, and the bag of assorted-shaped marshmallows marched on. Mr. Carson hadn't made his presence or wallet felt, and our table was in Siberia.

"I'm sorry I'm late. How are you?" I introduced or re-introduced myself to everyone at the table. Thank God Astrid was seated beside me. I needed at least one friend at the table. She seemed focused on Chuck Knight, who was also tossed from school because of my infamous list. He would be playing tennis for Wake Forest next year, though, and he was fine. I did not feel bad about him. Dave Kinsley and Jimmy Slatterfield were plotting together to my right after switching seats so that the Bellatini twins could sit together. Half Brazilian, half Italian, fashioned in Palm Beach and fine-tuned at St. Paul's, the Bellatinis were a Buckley boy's wet dream, each more bronzed and striking than the other. It was impossible to tell them apart. After introductions, I quickly matched their identities by their outfits and was safe from then on. Fernanda wore a strapless blue dress and sat to the left of Alicinha, with the pink shawl and silver hoop earrings, and both had impeccable posture and the conversational skills of a wall. I wanted to shake them. Their long, chestnut hair fell over bare, delicate shoulders. I stared as they twisted and arched their backs to see the ceremony up front. Dave's jaw was on the floor with eyes locked on the prize, but Slatterfield had a girlfriend at Vanderbilt and knocked back Greyhounds to resist temptation. The rest of the table was made up of Ed Weeks, Astrid's twenty-seven-year-old cousin who didn't say more than three words, and Christina Booth. Christina held court over the table with tales of her Asian studies major at Harvard. Nobody cared.

I could hardly see the "swans" as they lined up at the front of the room. It reminded me of a debutante ball. I was half expecting a group of acne-faced escorts to come up for the first dance when I saw someone else approach the microphone. A wiry wafer of a man floated up to the stage and hid behind the podium. From my distance I couldn't tell if he was walking or not. His graceful gait gave the impression that gravity did not apply to him at all. Perhaps he was once a fine ballroom dancer. I looked at my program and saw that the evening's master of ceremonies was Mr. Lewis van Wassel. He was rather tall but could not have been more than twenty-seven inches around the waist and twenty-five around the chest. Like a misshaped oblong egg, this man actually got skinnier with longitude. With a thirteen-year-old boy's pitch, the man cleared his throat and said, "Ladies and gentlemen." The crowd continued to murmur. "Ladies and gentlemen," he repeated, this time with a little bit of a third-grade art teacher's tone. Still no pause, so he began to tap his signet ring on the microphone and let out a catlike "pssssssshhhhhhhhhhhhhhhhhhh." I noticed his elongated fingers wrapped around the microphone's shaft two, maybe three times, like he tied them up in knots to stay out of the way.

"Good evening, and welcome to the Wildlife Conservation Society's ninety-seventh Charity Ball! I would like to thank the Bryan family, the Holts, the Tomensons, and the various other donors that helped make this evening a success."

I wondered how much you had to give for such a public form of gratitude.

"Behind me are twelve beautiful young ladies from our Junior Committee. Each represents the last living Amazonian Pharite birds left on this planet. The grazing and deforestation of the Brazilian rain forest has decimated this species' population, but with your help, we will increase this number tenfold by next year." A roaring applause. The music returned, the crowd awed, and each young lady crossed the stage making semi-graceful flapping motions with her arms. It was a little embarrassing, but I got it. Some looked terrified, some rolled their eyes, and some smiled to friends and family in the crowd. As they reached the center of the stage, they gave Mr. van Wassel a small scroll representing a pledge to the cause, turned to the crowd, and curtseyed as low as their five-hundred-dollar heels and high school lacrosse ankles would allow them. Some reached remarkably flexible positions, and I saw Dave and Jimmy exchange glances and take mental notes. One actually fell to one knee and looked mortified while van Wassel demonstrated physical difficulty picking her back up.

By the end of the procession, Mr. van Wassel's podium was full, and he had nowhere left to place the scrolls. He must have been holding at least five himself, and I thought, "That's why he was the man for the job. Those fingers!"

I could not have cared less about these insipid, inbred swans. All of my attention was on Layla. I spotted the back of her neck three tables away from mine and fixated on the arc of her shoulder for the rest of the meal, trying to catch a glimpse of the lines on her clavicle, drawing up to her delicate lips, lightly freckled nose, and hypnotizing eyes. Her table's attention was on her. Everyone seemed as captivated as I. I needed to talk to her without her dinner company. I could not bare the dialogue of a social background check in front of her. I could just hear it coming . . . "Where did you . . . prep?"

5

WHERE DID YOU PREP?

THE ASSHOLE QUESTION of the century, yet heard all too often, is "where did you prep?" A quick assessment at any cocktail party. Thank God I had the perfect answer, "Mather."

Mather Academy, a boarding school in the Berkshire Mountains whose school motto urged students to "Uphold your legacy." I felt at home as I walked down its maple-lined paths and looked to its blazing October hills. Colossal brick buildings with white Corinthian columns framed expansive green quadrangles spread throughout the campus. Before students arrived with tapestries, featherbeds, duvets, vacation pictures, flat-screen computer monitors, coffee table trunks, alcohol posters, and speakers, every student was situated with basic wood beds, bureaus, and desks. Swiss Army Knife engravings decorated the drawers and sides of each. Names you knew, names you associated with flooding the math department on prank day, skipping his senior year to play hockey for Harvard, or banging twenty-six girls during his time at Mather. The school had the ability to make you nostalgic for an era you never experienced. Any yearbook picture could have easily been from the twenties, fifties, or nineties. The faces didn't change. The facilities were better than any college I'd seen, and even the student body looked perfect. A teenage mass in pastels and blazers. I often felt I was in a great American novel just walking to class.

It was certainly a nice change from home, a chance to break away from my parents. My father, also Callum, ran a fund that bought and sold distressed companies in Latin America. He took over the company when Grandpapa, my mother's father, died years previous. Before that, he worked for Great Ridge Capital out of their São Paulo office. We lived there for the first eight years of my life. "Happy Valley," my parents used to call it. I didn't remember much, but the memories I had were pleasant ones. Rice and beans, juicy steaks, mouth-watering sweets, fresh fruits, the beach house in Juquei, tennis with Dad, my mom teaching my sister, Julia, and me to swim. My mom in general. She was happier down there. Before the drama, the moaning, the booze. Before the housekeeper's mental breakdown, before she ever screamed at my father. Anyway, yes, my father.

Dad worked around the clock and the globe, but the job suited his demanding nature. Julia and I were never allowed to quit anything in our lives. His sister, Liz, took an alternate approach to life and died of an overdose around the time I was born. My dad said that his father always let Liz quit whenever things got difficult. He was too "cushy" on her. Dad wasn't going to make the same mistake on me.

The summer after fourth grade, I was diagnosed with Lyme disease two days before my parents sent me to Vermont for tennis camp at Windridge (a veritable fresh-air fund for the Upper East Side and Southern Connecticut's youth). I remember not thinking much of that little tick bite and being thrilled about the summer ahead of me. Unfortunately, the antibiotic I was taking, Erythromycin, made me dangerously sensitive to the sun, so the camp nurse never let me out of my cabin. Like a normal nine-year-old, I disobeyed her to play tennis and soccer and learn how to interact with the opposite sex (this would be better than dancing school). By the end of the first week, I looked like I belonged in the burn unit at New York Presbyterian. My body was a horrific sight from my eyelids to the tips of my toes. My lips were swollen and full of blood blisters, my nose was raw, my ears felt like they were falling off, and even the palms of my hands were scorched. The other campers laughed at me, and I felt like a freak. I grew terribly homesick. I even wrote home bluff suicide notes with blood from picked scabs smeared on the margins, but my father would not let me quit.

He clearly had his ways, but one thing I thanked him for was pushing me to follow his footsteps at Mather. I loved the place. I was through with Saint Sebastian's and happy to be away from the City. I did not know it then, but I was glad to be away from my manic mother, the smell of her gown in the midst of a "funk," her wine-induced rants, and her pills. Not that he was ever around, but I was happy to escape from my father as well. It was time away from the boss.

Mather was formal summer camp, sheltered freedom. I couldn't have asked for more. Perhaps this is just nostalgia, but I believe I was actually liked there too. Not by everyone, mind you. Let's not get ahead of ourselves, but by most. You see, I had the place around my little finger and got away with murder. I had the zealous, overachieving, spirited "Mather Man" role down pat. I was Treasurer of the Latin American Student Coalition, along with Vice President of the Student Council; a member of the Student Activities Committee, Food Committee, and Prom Committee; and a photographer for the yearbook and the *Mather Mission*. I was also head of the Young Republican's Club and served as a member of GROH (Getting Rid of Homophobia), a legitimate walking, talking college application. I knew I had to roll in shit to get into school, and that is precisely what I did.

One of my biggest assets at Mather was my advisor, Chip Thomson. Thomson had gone to Mather himself and fell so in love with the place that, once he graduated, he came back and worked there ever since. His family came from wealth, and his wife came from more. It was never about money. He just loved Mather. A true "Mather Man," he was also one of the last teachers from the better generation, the kind that still wore a bowtie and told stories about how crazy our fathers were when they were there; the kind that realized life was a story and that primary characters wore tweed; they read, drank, and smoked; they used the same tests and curriculums year in and year out. They were the spirit of the school. These days, all the teachers were young socialists who stopped by for a couple of years before business school instead of joining the Peace Corps. Thomson was a rock. He had been there for thirty-five years and was still going strong. He treated his favorite guys like his best friends and his favorite girls like high school crushes, which had gotten him into a little trouble a while back.

Don't get me wrong, Thomson was a gentleman; I think that the times just moved a little too fast for him, and the politically correct world took over without anyone filling the poor guy in.

He used to be an English teacher and would always give preferential treatment to the popular guys and pretty girls. Whether this meant higher grades or signing off slips to skip class, it didn't matter. The point was that he was clearly showing favoritism, and the outcast nerds and bitter young faculty were not willing to overlook it anymore. It was a shame. He was a Mather institution, and the school ripped away his teaching position.

At least they didn't let him go, though. He was too loved. So, they reinvented his role and made him Head of the Dining Hall. At Mather we had sit-down lunches five days a week and sit-down dinners on Mondays and Wednesdays. These were times when all six hundred students gathered under one roof in class dress and sat at assigned tables with other students and faculty. Thomson ate it up as he became more of an icon. The Dining Hall was his stage, a place where he would control the entire school for multiple hours every day. Students soon started calling him the Czar, as he ruled the dining hall like his empire. It was a massive room with fifty-foot ceilings and walls lined with wood plaques engraved by every Mather graduate since 1797.

Every senior was forced to take an elective in carpentry. In this period, they would work on their own two-by-two plaque to leave behind as their mark on the school. I recall seeing everything from engravings in the shape of Nantucket, to family crests, to various peace-oriented themes from the sixties, to a confederate flag, and even a Black Panther fist. I never knew what I would put on mine. It was a subject that had kept me up on various nights. I wanted a memorable legacy.

Anyway, Thomson was the man who made table assignments at meals, he was the guy who decided who was a first waiter (who set tables) and second waiter (who cleared them), and he was the person in charge of grace and announcements. This is where Thomson started helping me out.

Thomson had interviewed me when I first came to look at Mather because the regular admissions officer was out of town for a funeral. This was pure luck because it turned into the best interview I'll ever have. We spoke about girls, New York, the Rangers, the Knicks, tennis, and basically everything I enjoyed discussing. So, when I came to Mather as a freshman, he looked out for me from the very beginning. I was able to hand select my dining partners, I was never a waiter, and I didn't even have to show up for sit-down meals if I wasn't in the mood. Sometimes he would call me into his office to help him set up amusing tables. We once assigned a table filled with the smallest girls in the school and the offensive line of the football team. Another table was made up of couples that had dated the year before and were no longer together. It was all in good fun, and my friendship with Thompson helped me out on multiple occasions, and not just in the dining hall.

Thomson was also the JV football and hockey coach, as well as the Varsity track coach. At Mather, you either had to play a sport, be in the play, or do community service every afternoon. Thomson always saved me a spot on his rosters to be his "manager," meaning that I would go down to the track or fields, drop off his clipboard, shake his hand, and take off for the afternoon. I know it does not sound like much right now, but trust me, free time was a precious luxury at boarding school.

My buddies and I thought ourselves untouchable. Most of my friends were big-time athletes, all getting recruited for hockey and lacrosse. When you're at a school like Mather, where sports mean everything, athletes get the royal treatment. My other friends were either second- or third-generation Mather, had donated some building, or both. Put us all together with my bullshit "Go Mather" façade, and we had the school by the balls.

6

TYPHOON

"TIM, GRAB A BATCH of A.P. on your way back."

"What's that?" asked the boy from West Hartford in khakis and a blazer over his fleece. Tim was a periphery member of our freshman circle of friends.

"Mix for Arnold Palmers! You're going to the dining hall, right? So grab a pitcher and fill it up half iced tea and half lemonade. We need a mixer for tonight."

I smiled at my friends, Branson and Curtis, across the common room. The school just made it too easy. Mather was a veritable country club, and we were raucous members. There were mazes of storage rooms in dorm basements where we'd sit on old trunks and stay up through the night playing poker and backgammon for cash. On spring weekends we'd take nine irons and hit golf balls between the uprights on the football field. Paddle legends were made on cold winter nights in the cage. If fortunate enough, it was fairly easy to sneak over to the girls' dorms for a little action. Windows had no locks or alarms, and the only night security was a team of three golf carts patrolling the school's brick paths. If you were wily, or fast, you were safe. Even immature pranks were fun. We once used masking tape to press down the button on five air freshener spray cans and threw them into a classmate's room for "fumigation." Windows and doors sealed shut. When poor Charlie Perkins came back, he wasn't able to sleep in his room for two days, and his sheets forever smelled like a disinfected airport bathroom. My personal favorite was "Tranbaugh's typhoon."

It was about ten o'clock on a Monday night my freshman spring. Thomas Longview banged on my door.

"Littlefield, do you still have any air freshener from your 'fumigations' on Perkins?"

"Yeah," I laughed, "Costco sells them by the thirty," and I pulled up my duvet cover to show him the package I had bought on my last run into town.

"Sick." He reached under my bed to grab one. "Let's go."

I knew exactly what he was up to. Thomas was an old friend from Saint Sebastian's. We'd been in the same class since we were seven, and he was one of my best friends. Believe it or not, he was actually the best athlete in our class back in the City. I think he was a little put off when he was cut from varsity wrestling at Mather freshman year because he kind of gave up sports in general and started smoking a lot of pot. He was still talented as hell and ripped up ultimate frisbee games. He was probably also the best FIFA soccer PlayStation player in the dorm.

Smoking was about as normal as drinking for our group at Mather. There were a bunch of sophomore potheads in our dorm freshman year, and they showed us the ropes in no time, so it wasn't a big surprise that this was going on, but I remember feeling hesitant following him down the hall that night. I had a bio quiz the next day and wanted to get my grades in order.

I walked into Longview's room and saw Chuck Knight and Curtis Black wrestling on the couch. Both of them wore flip-flops, khaki shorts, button-down shirts, and ties. I saw two blazers on the floor and guessed that this match had just begun. That reminded me that my blazer was still stuffed in my backpack, but I would take it out later. Longview locked his door after him, pulled a small bag out of the back of his desk drawer, and took out a plastic vial.

"Let's do this, you idiots. Purple Haze. Sensi Seed delivery boys."

"Is there anything you can't get delivered in New York?" Chuck asked from the grips of Curtis' headlock. Chuck was from Darien, not exactly a stretch from the City, but out of delivery range.

"Your hot suburban mother," Curtis responded while squeezing Chuck's neck in his own armpit.

Thomas smiled as he pushed Black off of Knight. Curtis Black was also from the City and had gone to Buckley. We knew him from wrestling games and dances but only became friends once we got to Mather. He was one of the few freshmen to make the lacrosse team and liked everyone to know it.

"Sorry man. I'm going to bounce on this one. Coach is riding me these days. Varsity athlete thing. You guys wouldn't understand."

"Come on, Black. Not like you're ever going to play this year. Sit the fuck down," Chuck pleaded.

"Not worried about the games, man. It's tomorrow's practice. Smith literally hates me."

It was true. Coach Smith hated Black. Probably because he was from New York and went to Buckley. He thought city kids were pansies and gave them a hard time more often than not.

Curtis closed the door.

"Guess it's just us," Longview said, relocking the door.

"Knight, turn on the fan." Chuck was one step ahead of him and closed the window shades as he turned Thomas's window fan on the High Exhaust setting. I took a towel and put it along the crack between Thomas's door and the floor. Thomas then threw me an empty Gatorade bottle, a box of dryer sheets, and a penknife.

"Hit bottle."

"Got it." Give me a sec. I pulled the blade out of the gadget with my fingernails, which needed to be cut, and then made a quarter-sized hole in the bottom of the bottle. After stuffing the hole from the other side with two dryer sheets, I threw it to Chuck.

"All set." Chuck blew into the Gatorade bottle and Thomas smelt the other side.

"Wow. If it cures Knight's breath, then we have nothing to worry about!" Chuck punched Thomas in the shoulder.

Thomas finally pulled out a small glass piece and a lighter from a pocket in his T. Anthony weekend bag and packed the bowl from his vial.

Thomas took the first hit, held it, and then exhaled through the "hit bottle," which he held up to the window fan.

"Pass the . . . 'chips,'" Chuck said in code. Thomas passed him the piece, and Knight followed suite. As my turn came around, I remember feeling trapped and wishing we could get it over with quickly. No opening the door at that point, though.

We were in it together. I took a hit, held it, and then violently coughed toward the fan.

"Shut the fuck up!" Thomas whisper-yelled as he punched me in the arm. Chuck smashed a pillow in my face to conceal the noise.

"Sorry guys." I didn't smoke that often and tried to stifle embarrassment. We went around twice more, and I took smaller hits to control my reactions.

After putting everything away, changing shirts, applying Visine, and gargling mouthwash, we sat in Thomas's room stoned as hell and dying for food. Ordering delivery would mean we would have to wait by the entrance and risk seeing our dorm master, Mr. Tranbaugh, so that was out of the question, but I had an idea.

I left the room and walked to the second floor to William Kim's room. William was a Korean freshman and heir to the Choi automotive fortune. I walked into his room and heard him screaming Korean into a cell phone and then saw him spike it on the bed. Nobody had cell phones at Mather yet.

"Woah. Where did you get that?" I asked.

"Piece of shit Japanese phone," William responded. "Can't hear shit on the other end. Can't even fight with girlfriend."

"Everything okay, William? I'm sorry man." William sat on the bed and put his head in his hands. I noticed he wore a Rolex on both of his wrists and that a mass amount of product kept his perfectly parted helmet-like hair in place.

"Pain in the ass, man. I've been in this shit country since I was eight." William had gone to Hawkstream, an all-boy elementary boarding school, before Mather. This sounded intense, even to me. "I'm forgetting Korean and still don't speak English. Slipping through cracks, man."

While hindsight is 20/20, at the time I could only laugh.

"What the fuck, man? You think that funny? I also failing Geometry. Fucking Tranbaugh don't like Asians. I know it. You stoned, white boy? Just want my noodles, huh?"

He was right. I wanted his Korean noodle care packages. William's closet was filled with delicious insta-noodle boxes from Korea, and he had grown all too accustomed to morons like me mooching off him.

"Go head. Take them. Eat up."

"Sorry, William. I really hope you feel better."

"Yeah, yeah."

Longview, Knight, and I sat in Longview's room playing video games, grading the freshman girls in the roster book, and eating noodles. I looked down at my soup and realized I was screwed for bio the next day but felt still worse for William.

"You know what, guys?" I asked. "I have an idea. Follow me. We're typhooning Tranbaugh." Longview and Knight gave perplexed looks to each other.

I grabbed Longview's school-issued garbage can, took it to the bathroom, and filled it up in the shower. The hall had caught on, and Curtis helped me carry it back to the hallway.

"Wait a second, I have an idea," Curtis said as he unzipped his pants. The whole hall moaned.

"What the fuck, man? Put your dick away!"

"Just a second." Curtis scrunched his eyes and made a face like he was constipated. "Here it comes." He let out a short stream of urine into the garbage. Everyone laughed.

Curtis and I carried the can down the hallway trying not to spill the water and pee all over ourselves. We leaned it gently against Mr. Tranbaugh's door and held in our laughter. Everyone else had made their way back to their rooms and stuck their heads out to view the action. Curtis and I looked at each other, silently counted to three, knocked hard on the door, and sprinted back to our rooms. Twenty doors slammed shut within three seconds. The silence was thick until we heard the turn of a door handle and the crash of the garbage, water, and urine, all over Mr. Tranbaugh's feet and vestibule.

"WHAT THE HELL?"

His door slammed, and twenty freshman boys howled themselves to sleep behind closed doors.

"IDIOTS," We heard Tranbaugh yell from within his apartment.

As we grew older (and had more access to IDs), our diversions became increasingly centered on drinking. We got wasted before dances, hockey games, even class. The more risk, the better. You'd think that the school would have us locked down pretty hard, but it was a joke. Water bottles filled with vodka, iced tea bottles filled with whiskey, and Gatorade bottles filled with rum; my senior year dresser was a veritable bar. Nothing I am proud of. I really should not have been screwing around so much, considering I was on probation from my first slip sophomore year.

7

STRIKE ONE

WE DRANK WARM VODKA that night. Sophomore winter. Branson Jones, one of my best friends and hall-mates in Phillips Dormitory, and I took a taxi into Yellowtown (Mather's trailer park excuse for a town and domestic abuse capital of the northeast) to find supplies for the evening. Branson had also gone to Windridge, but we only reconnected when we arrived at Mather as freshmen. I looked about twelve years old, and even though Branson was six foot four, his boyish face could not pass for twenty-one either. We stood in the parking lot of the liquor store for about two hours searching for a pawn.

Our cheeks burned, our snot froze, and we could hardly feel our toes. I hadn't felt that deep a chill since 6:00 AM hockey practices as a kid. I remembered my dad coming up behind me on the bench in attempt to fire me up. He would grab my face mask, shake my frame around, and preach about how he wanted me after the puck like a "bat out of hell!" I hated hockey.

Dad got the point that it wasn't my sport after my embarrassing performance at the Junior Islander hockey camp. It must
have been negative twenty degrees. I could not stand it anymore
and decided to make a bolt. Ten minutes after face off, I was in
full hockey equipment and skates, bursting into tears, and sprinting toward route 25A. I still remember the sound of my skates on
the concrete of the parking lot. To get me back on the ice, Dad
convinced Brian Trottier, Islander Hall of Famer and head of the
camp, to come out and carry me back in. Beats an autograph, huh?

Yellowtown, Massachusetts, was just as cold that day. Still,
we were determined young Mather men. I flipped up and buttoned the corduroy collar of my Barbour jacket over my chin
and dug my hands deep into its ripped pockets.

"Grab me if someone comes, dude, I can't deal with this
wind," said Branson, and he turtle-buried his head deep into his
beige fleece.

After a few hours, we finally spotted a sure thing. This gentleman was one of the sketchier characters I had ever come across.
He walked as if he were falling asleep, rocking back and forth,
and every time it seemed as if he was going to loose his balance,
he would twitch back up as if someone had just shocked him
with static. His black jeans were tucked into his knee-high army
boots, and his Carhartt jacket was ripped in several places. He
had a goatee and slick, greasy black hair, all of which made his
rough, ghostlike face stand out even more. I nudged Branson.

"Let's do this."

I knew this would be our last hope. We could not stay
much longer.

"Hey man," I called out. He kept walking.

"Want to make a quick forty bucks?" He stopped and awoke,

eyes lighting up slowly like an old television. We probably re-
kindled some sort of meth addiction for the guy, but that was
his business.

"What do you fucks need?" A slithering raspy voice.

We told him there would be cash waiting with us in the
parking lot if he bought us two handles of vodka. He disappeared into the store for a long ten minutes.

"I bet he left, dude. Back door and bolted with our money.
We're fucked," grumbled Branson.

"No way. He wants the extra forty."

The liquor store's glass door finally opened, and our friend
returned across the parking lot with two bottles of the cheapest
crap he could find. Aristocrat Vodka . . .

"Great," said Branson. "Real classy. No change, I assume."

"No. Shit's expensive. Where is the rest?"

We gave him the tip and didn't care. We were set for the night.

Back at school, Branson, this other buddy of ours named
Josh Crawford, and I met up in my room around eight thirty.
Josh was kind of a whack job. He had the potential to be a solid
student but loathed his parents so much that he turned his attention to hippy jam bands and mushrooms to spite them.

Once I woke up at four in the morning to the sounds of
Pink Floyd blasting from the hallway. I followed the noise into
the bathroom and found Josh butt naked doing pushups on the
linoleum floor. It was February, and the bathroom window was
wide open with four cigarette butts sitting on the ledge. Josh
must have known I was there, but he did not look at me or say
a word. He just kept on with his pushups. Cold sweat ran all
over his face. It was the type of thing I knew not to bring up to
anyone. He came into my room at 2:00 AM the next night.

"It just sets me into a trance, man. Can't explain it, but it takes me away from this shit hole for awhile, and I can't complain about *that*, bro." With that, he closed the door and let me roll back to sleep.

Branson, Josh, and I met up in my room, locked the door, closed the window shade, and opened my trunk to find the two treasured, lukewarm bottles of Aristocrat. My floor master, Mr. Thune, was chaperoning the evening's Valentine's Day dance, so we were not too worried about getting a knock on my door. But still, we knew that we had to move quickly. We each threw back about five or six shots. I then put the bottles back in the trunk beneath three blankets. After locking the trunk, I gargled mouthwash for thirty seconds, took a stick of gum, and casually left the dorm as I had seen my mother do countless times back home.

We strutted across the snowy quad, confident and smirking, with the empty warmth of vodka in our stomachs. I busted through the dining room doors, spotted the three chaperones, and placed myself in the opposite corner.

The dance was a pretty typical Mather party. A local DJ was playing Top 40 dance hits, and nobody was on the floor except for the ethnics in one corner and the cute freshman girls in the other. I wasn't in the mood for dancing, though, as I didn't want to give off any hint that I was drunk. Branson, Josh, and I leaned against a wall and pointed out our favorite freshman girls in their little cupid-like outfits.

"Oh my god would I hit that . . ." Josh drooled.

"Which one?" I asked.

"That Asian chick, man." Josh fixated his gaze on her.

"Seriously? Have you ever hooked up with one?" Branson followed.

"Give me a break. Josh hasn't hooked up with a brunette before. One step at a time." I laughed.

"No, no I don't think so. But my brother has, though, dude. They are supposed to be total freaks. Screamers." Josh made a V with his fingers and stuck his tongue out in between.

"Go talk to her, man." Branson punched Josh on the shoulder.

"Fuck it, dude. She's a tease."

"Come on, you pussy!"

"No, maybe later."

"You guys are morons. Let's move." I laughed, and gestured toward the teacher that had drifted slowly in our direction throughout the conversation.

The dance got old quickly, so we headed over to the Store. The Store was a place with TVs, arcade games, a jukebox, and a quick-order grill where students could hang out. It was our boarding school Cheers, if you will. Soon enough, underclassmen curfew rolled around, so Branson, Josh, and I headed back to Phillips.

When we got back to the dorm, the faculty master on duty, Mr. Hiddlebindle, told us that Ms. Clementeen had been by the dorm looking for us.

"Not good, gentlemen," he said, in an uncle's tone of disapproval.

Ms. Clementeen was one of the school's deans and was known for busting kids on a regular basis. I saw Branson and Josh's faces go pale, but I gave them a stern look.

"Deny everything," I whispered as we walked up the stairs.

We each went to our respective rooms and waited for the inevitable. I killed time downloading music, checking my email, and playing video games. Finally, I heard her sharp knock on the door.

Clementeen entered in her notorious black pants suit. A skin-colored mole shivered above the left side of her upper lip as she prepared to speak. She looked down at me sitting at my desk.

"Where is the vodka, Callum?"

I looked back with a blank stare.

"Give me the vodka."

"I think this is a misunderstanding, Ms. Clementeen. I don't—"

"A member of the faculty saw you exchanging money for a brown paper bag in the parking lot of a liquor store," she cut me off coldly, annunciating the end of each word and holding onto pauses in between.

I denied it.

"Branson and I went to Friendly's for lunch today, but we definitely didn't buy liquor."

She pushed back her bobbed hair so that the darkness covered her stray whites and responded, "Your friends have already admitted everything, Mr. Littlefield. You are only making this worse. Do not *lie* to me."

Mather's honor code had a one-strike policy for lying. I didn't buy it, but I remained silent just in case. No point in digging deeper. The room remained silent.

"Well then, if you're not going to speak, I'm going to have to ask you to stand outside your door while I search your room."

The very next day, I found myself in front of a disciplinary committee of my peers. We met in the boardroom in the library. Most of the committee was made up of friends (friends who I had also broken rules with), but this was a pretty black-and-white case, and these hearings had faculty supervision. Three-day suspension and probation through graduation. This was a standard punishment for drinking, but I was mortified.

I walked into the school meeting the day before having to leave to serve my suspension and tried to buck up for the task in front of me. I felt excited to speak in front of the school, yet doomed for every moment after that.

I sat in the back right corner section of the auditorium with the rest of the sophomore class.

"TWO THOU-SAND! TWO THOU-SAND! TWO THOU-SAND," the seniors began to chant from up front.

"ZE-RO ONE! ZE-RO ONE! ZE-RO ONE!" went the juniors.

My classmates stood up around me and began "ZE-RO TWO! ZE-RO TWO! ZE-RO TWO," but I remained in my chair and rehearsed the lines I was planning to use. I had written them down but did not want to use any notes. That morning, I had practiced in front of the full-length mirror in my room but kept a low voice so that nobody would hear me as they passed by in the hall. It wouldn't be cool to practice a student council resignation, but I wanted to look cool up there.

"ZE-RO THREE, ZE-RO THREE," came the freshmen with half the force of the other classes. They were soon booed back into their seats.

"Calm down, calm down everyone." Mr. Ponzer was entering into his tenth year as Mather's headmaster, and it was rumored to be his last. Ponzer was an overweight man with tired eyes, ruddy cheeks, and a bulbous nose. His receding hairline gave him a distinguished look, which made up for his often-disheveled appearance. Whether it be a mistucked shirt, an uneven tie, or a ketchup stain on his houndstooth jacket, Ponzer always had something off.

The meeting started off with faculty announcements.

"It has come to my attention that some students are not

clearing their tables at walk-through meals. Leaving your food for someone else to pick up is unacceptable behavior. You are young adults, and you should be acting like that. I don't know if you act this way in your own homes, but it is not acceptable at Mather," said Mr. Hanson.

"Thank you, Mr. Hanson. Are there any other announcements from the faculty? Ms. Dominguez."

A young first-year Spanish teacher approached the front of the room.

"OWE OWE. Arriba Arriba!" came the catcalls from boys in the balcony.

"That is enough, men," glared Ponzer as he gave Ms. Dominguez the microphone.

"Hola estudantes!"

"ME GUSTA!" came another call, and Ms. Dominguez smiled.

"I am hosting a paella dinner this Friday in my apartment on Armstong three. Please sign up in the mail room if you are interested."

"I'll be there!" someone yelled, and everyone laughed.

Mr. Ponzer took back the microphone and motioned for student announcements. "Serena, do you have a word from Students' Activity Committee?

Most of the male student body hummed "SAAAC," lifting their hands in the air, gesturing the cupping of a scrotum sac. Serena Schleifenheiser smiled and blushed as she walked down the aisle to announce this week's social activities.

"Yah Yah Rena!" yelled Vickie Vietor, Serena's roommate, from the crowd.

"Thank you, Mr. Ponzer. Hi guys! This Friday, we have a bus leaving for the Springfield Mall at 6:00 PM and returning by

10:00. We will also be showing *Braveheart* and *Mermaids* in the science center theatres. Eighties cover band Orange Crush will be playing in the Lavely center at 8:00 PM on Saturday, so dig up your leggings, denim, neon, and scrunchies!"

"Thank you Serena. Cheerleaders?" The room went pitch black, and the crowd began to scream. Cheerleaders at Mather were not girls with pom poms and skirts. They were traditionally the eleven most popular and athletic seniors. One junior was chosen each year, and he or she would be head cheerleader the following year and had the responsibility to refill his or her roster. They wore white whaling sweaters with green Ms on them and carried old-fashioned megaphones to be heard across campus. They led every pep rally and fired up the school for big games. Mather's hockey team had a grudge match against Exeter that weekend, and the crowd was expecting some sort of announcement.

My eyesight adjusted when I heard a low Gregorian chant underneath the screams from the crowd in the darkness, and the cheerleaders processed down the center aisle two by two. It appeared six of them were carrying a casket and the rest held candles and hummed to the low mysterious chants coming from a boom box in the back of the room. I would have normally loved such a spectacle, but I wished that I were in that casket. As they passed by my row, I noticed that the casket had an Exeter banner draped over it. The twelve cheerleaders placed the casket down and lined up across the entire stage holding their respective candles underneath their faces. Tyler Canner, head cheerleader, stepped forward.

"On Saturday, January 20, in the two thousandth year of our Lord . . . EXETER . . . WILL . . . DIE!" The crowd stood up and roared. The rest of the cheerleaders grabbed their megaphones from behind the curtain and banged their metal mouthpieces against the ground, chanting, "AGA CHEE, AGA CHA, AGA CHEE-CHEE CHA-CHA-CHA, BOOMBA BOOMBA SISCUM BA, MATHER MATHER—RAH RAH!"

The lights came back on, and Mr. Ponzer tried to quiet down the now-electric crowd. "Okay, everyone, okay. Quiet down. We still have one more announcement from the Disciplinary Committee." The noise came to a halt, and I sank in my seat.

Whittaker Campbell, editor of the *Mission,* straight-A student, and head of the disciplinary committee walked to the front of the room. He adjusted his oversized glasses and pushed back his brown premature comb-over.

"Oooooooh," whispered some of the seniors loud enough to hear. I felt like hundreds of eyes were on me.

"The Disciplinary Committee met yesterday to discuss the case of three sophomore boys breaking Mather's drug and alcohol policy. These three young men will be suspended for three days and placed on probation through the remainder of their time at Mather. As an officer of the student council, Callum Littlefield will now address the school."

For some reason I almost giggled, but I held my mouth tight, shuffled across my row, and walked to the front of the room. I looked at the six hundred students in front of me and took a deep breath.

"Hi everyone." I peered up at the crowd and saw some of the senior guys right in front of me smile. An uneasy energy pulsed through the room, but most of the faces I saw looked completely blank. Open unengaged eyes and cracked mouths with zero expression. "I'm up here to apologize for my actions. As the vice president of the sophomore class, I have let you down as a leader and as a representative. I did not consider the consequences of my actions, and I deliberately broke my oath to the council. I hereby resign from my position."

I handed the microphone back to Mr. Ponzer and walked back to my seat as he closed up the meeting. The audience did not react, and in a way, I remember feeling tough and enjoying the attention. I wondered what girls would think of me and if this would help me score. Some people asked me if I was okay after the meeting and others patted me on the back, but I doubt anyone really cared. Midterms were around the corner.

It wasn't until I packed my bags for home that the meeting's energy wore off and the pain hit me again. I thought about the future, and it killed me. I'd never fucked up before. I was perfect, right? Mr. Untouchable.

I cried in my room at home throughout the entire suspension. What would I do? What were people saying? Could I transfer? I guess I could always go to a Salisbury or something. I couldn't imagine life outside of Mather. My mother imitated my behavior and also sat in her room for days. A dark cloud came over her, similar to ones I'd seen before. She thought it was her fault. I could hear her moan and cry from my room. I'd pass her lying on the couch and see her tear-smeared mascara, and it crushed me.

She told me not to pick up the house phone lines so that nobody would know I had been sent home. "It's embarrassing." My father was away on business, but you can bet I received a few terrifying phone calls from him.

"Callum, you let us down. What is your plan now?"

"I don't know."

"Well you better start thinking about it. How are you going to turn this around?"

They never had to go through this with Julia.

"I want a typed letter on my desk by Monday with an explanation and a plan looking forward."

I just wanted to get back to Mather, and three days felt like an eternity.

8

THE PRETZEL

"CALLUM! I STILL have not danced with my godbrother!"

I had spent my meal ignoring my company and trying to steal glances from Layla. Guests finished their crab cakes, filet mignon, and asparagus, and I threw back my fourth glass of wine and worked up my courage to make a move. Shit, Astrid.

Okay. Setback. I had to dance with my godsister. I could not be rude to her. She was such a sweetheart. We never had anything romantic between us or anything, but I always thought she was a great girl. Besides, I love dancing after a few drinks, and Astrid could move. I glanced at Chuck and caught him staring at Fernanda. He wouldn't mind.

The Lester Lanin orchestra was playing a "Twist and Shout/ La Bamba" medley, and Astrid and I were tearing it up.

Layla was dancing with another guy across the floor. Shit. It was Duncan Dawson. A much better dancer than I was, but kind of a dork and probably just a friend. I had to step it up. She was energetic, yet poised and elegant. I tried to spin Astrid in her direction so I could show off my moves.

The band was cooking, and the "country club mother" dancing was in full effect. Women of all ages were kicking off their heels and doing aerobics all over the dance floor. For some reason, 90 percent of preppy women danced like this after two glasses of wine. I have no idea why, but they just lacked rhythm. Half of them looked like they were working on their volleys, while the other half appeared to be having seizures. Oh, and spinning. They couldn't get enough spinning. It's like it was the only move they knew, so they kept doing it over and over again, often completely out of control. A diamond and pearl tornado.

Anyway, I was about to pull my most impressive dancing school move, "the Pretzel," with Astrid when—UMPF!—one woman actually elbowed me square in the sternum. Not only did she knock the wind out of me, but she also forced Astrid to bump a young girl off of the dance floor and almost crush an escaped parrot sitting on a nearby table. Tears, caws, and screaming everywhere. Negative attention. Bad. The seven-year-old girl had a powerful cry for such a petite young lady. She drowned out the bird as it hopped back up to table twelve's breadbasket. *Make it better, Callum.* I immediately helped the girl to her feet, patted her hair, dried off her tears with my handkerchief, and made sure that she was okay.

The girl wasn't hurt, but she was upset because the crash had made someone spill red wine all over her new flower-print party dress. As Astrid dried her off, I tried to cheer her up by getting her a Shirley Temple with extra cherries. I could tell she was still a little shaken, so I took her hand and had her lead me to her parents across the tent. I introduced myself, apologized again, and was about to turn away when I heard her tiny voice ask:

"Will you dance with me too?"

I could not say no to such a precious little thing, especially after I had almost stepped on her, so we went out and did a rendition of the Charleston to "Brown Eyed Girl." After thanking Carolina for our dance, I turned my attention back to Layla and her dance partner. She smiled and laughed as her partner dipped her and led her across the room. Who was that guy? I was invisible, and I wondered if she would want anything to do with me. My exit story had become pretty infamous on the boarding school circuit, and I'm sure it had been twisted for the worse.

9

SENIOR SPRING

MY SECOND, AND FINAL, strike at Mather came in the prime of my senior spring, just a few weeks before graduation. Timing could not have been worse. I was already into Penn, and grades were inconsequential. Dad actually seemed proud of me for following his Quaker footsteps and had begun telling me about his club, St. As, and all of the fun I had ahead of me. I had created an alternate study project for the semester that allowed me to spend my spring mapping out the Mather River for fly-fishing spots. I only had two real classes a day. I'd spend most of my time splashing around on the riverbanks and not doing much at all. My buddies and I had discovered our own little secret swimming beach, past the rapids and upstream about two hundred yards from where everybody else bathed. There, we could do whatever we pleased. Most of the guys went there to get high, but my personal distraction was to set up a tree ladder and rope swing.

We would often go down there at night, either before check-in or at the wee hours of the morning, rip off our clothes, sprint across the football field, and do perfect, high-arching swan dives off of the mud banks and into the crisp, flowing water. It was best when the air was warm and you could collapse on the soft grass of the athletic fields, look up at the stars, and pick the river mud out of your toes.

Four years earlier, on my first drive up to Mather, my Dad told me stories about this great rope swing his old gang built. They too had found their own little cove where they hung a rope off of a branch so that they could literally fly into the river. A week later, he sent me a black-and-white picture of himself inverted in a perfect pike position over the mighty Mather. They too used to sneak down there in the middle of warm September and May nights and spend hours bathing under the moonlight. The valley was theirs, and they felt like young kings. In a sense, they were. I wanted to recreate this memory.

I also spent a great amount of my senior spring with my ex-girlfriend, Michelle. I used to think that Michelle Winthorp was the ideal girl, a southern belle from Nashville. She had long blonde hair, seductive blue eyes, and a terrific figure. Michelle's skin always looked as if she had spent the prior day at sea. Perfectly sun kissed. She was a year behind me, but you couldn't really tell, since she always hung out with my crowd and had the confidence of a senior. She drove guys crazy as a freshman, walking around campus in her tiny Lilly Pulitzer skirts. She always acted naive and almost foolish, but like most private-school only-daughters, she worked hard and was competitive as hell. Her grades reflected this nature.

By the time she was a junior, Michelle had abandoned some of her girl-next-door persona and secured her position with the popular girls in her class from New York and Greenwich. Like her peers, she now pushed the limits of class dress with button-down blouses over school-issued sweatpants and Manolo Blahnik heels. She smelled like expensive perfume and she now smoked cigarettes. The innocence underneath her attempt to fit in drove me wild. I fell hard for her that spring. Anyway, I guess she had a thing for me too. Maybe because I was a senior, from the City, and in the right crowd. I didn't know or care. Discounting past summer flings and elementary school romances, she was my first legitimate relationship.

When I wasn't in the music practice rooms trying to get past second base with Michelle, I was jealously fighting with her about her constant filtrations with the post grad jocks.

"Bobby is just a friend, Cal. Relax."

"Guys aren't friends with girls they don't want to hook up with. Give me a break."

"Well, I can't help that . . . I don't like him like that."

And I'd see her cheering on the baseball team the following Saturday as well.

My feelings toward Michelle hovered around youthful passion and possessive jealousy.

But she was not my only focus that spring. My parents kept a country house upstate in Millbrook. My sister loved horseback riding, and my parents enjoyed the silence. I thought it was boring. Over the years, I became friends with a local kid by the name of Alex Cole. Al was a year ahead of me, but we were always great buddies. He had gone to Westminster and was a stud lacrosse player there. Not the brightest kid, but I guess he somehow used his athletic ability to get himself into Amherst. Conveniently, Amherst is only twenty minutes from Mather, so whenever I needed something, Al was there. The drunken shit-show that was our senior fall was all thanks to him. Day after day, he would show up

with more booze. It's amazing we got away with it. Al was definitely making a profit off of all of this too, so he didn't mind. One
day, he told me that he had recently found a cheap weed hook-up.
As most of my friends were halfway to rehab and had funds coming out of their asses, I thought this was a great opportunity.

My business began right after Christmas vacation senior
year. I started buying eighths of some crap probably grown in
a Burlington basement for forty-five dollars each and sold them
for sixty. I felt sort of bad ripping off my friends, but considering they had nowhere else to go, I had to take advantage of the
opportunity. Dad would have been proud. I had a spreadsheet
in my wallet with accounts receivable and everything. Al and I
were really starting to make a lot of money on this. My client
base had grown to about twenty, and I soon became so busy
that I started skipping class on a frequent basis.

Mather had this system where if you missed a class, you got
four accountability points. If you received over sixteen points
in a trimester, you got something called restrictions, which was
basically boarding school detention. I had only received about
twelve APs my entire career at Mather, so I wasn't going to start
getting them now. I'd simply go to the student health center,
put on my boyish charm, and plead with the nurses to sign off
my points claiming Montezuma's revenge. I always thought that
diarrhea worked nicely, because it sort of put the nurses in an
awkward position, you know? Especially when you used words
like *explosive*. The entire infirmary probably thought I suffered
from irritable bowel syndrome.

Teachers started getting suspicious though. One May afternoon, just a few weeks before graduation, Mr. Thompson left a
note in my mailbox.

Callum,
Please stop by the house this afternoon to chat.

Mr. T

I walked into his house on Main Street without knocking, and he told me to have a seat in his library. I didn't think anything of it. Black-and-white pictures of him in younger form graced the walls. One New England landscape oil painting hung over the leather couch with needlepoint throw pillows in its corners. "It's hard to be humble when you went to Mather," read one pillow; another said, "Gardeners have the best dirt."

"Can I fix you a sandwich or anything, Callum? How about a soda?"

"No, thank you, sir. What's going on?"

"Cal," he said, as he straightened his tie, "We just had the student review yesterday, and, as I'm sure you know, that is when we go through every student in the school and discuss if anyone is having any . . . issues."

Crazy system, huh? All of the teachers sat down in the round once a semester and just threw out every piece of gossip, hallway rumor, or secret they had heard about anyone or anything onto the table. Their sources stretched from overhearing students in the locker rooms to kids snitching on others. Everything and anyone was game.

"Yeah, I mean, yes. I know." I said. "Is anything wrong? Did my name come up?"

"Well, Callum, it seems that you have not really gone to a full day of classes in about a week."

"Yes, sir, I know. I really haven't been feeling well."

He smiled and went on.

"The thing is, Callum, many teachers have also seen you disappearing into the woods down by the river quite a bit, and they are suspicious, especially Ms. Clementeen. You've only got a few weeks left around here, and it'd really be a shame if you threw away all these years of hard work for some cheap thrill."

Cheap thrill?! Even Mr. Thompson thought I was a fuck-up. Well, I guess rightly so, but still, I had to smooth this over.

"I completely understand, Mr. Thompson, but you really don't have to worry about me. I guess I was just getting a little lazy, with it being senior spring and all, but I definitely have not been breaking any rules. You are welcome to come down with your children and try the swing out any time. I promise, that's all that I've been doing."

"You're sure? You're almost there."

Where? I thought. Where the hell was I going?

"I promise, sir. Things are fine." He smiled.

"Okay then, Cal. Off you go. Thanks for coming in."

"No problem, Mr. Thompson. Have a good one," I said as I left the room.

I was a modern Eddie Haskell when I felt like it. I was still worried about Ms. Clementeen's suspicions. She was known for screwing seniors over. She once even prevented a kid from graduating with his class just because he was smoking cigarettes in a math classroom five nights before commencement. Fire code *and* tobacco infringements, she called it.

Well, I completely ignored Mr. Thompson's warning and went on with my business. I'd attend more class. No problem. No more slip-ups. I was untouchable.

10

THE LIST

"AND HERE IS OUR final contestant. Hello Callum." Ms. Clementeen said through her crooked teeth and thin lips.

Two nights after my meeting with Thompson, I walked into the dorm for check-in and I saw my entire hall sitting in the common room.

"Please, sit down." She paced the room tapping a pen on her notebook. I looked at the frayed pockets of her black pants suit and wondered if it was the same one she wore when she busted me sophomore year.

"Hellooo Ms. Clementeen," I said in a mocking tone. "Did we win some sort of special hall feed? I didn't know our GPA was that high." That got a chuckle out of the guys. We were a "bad" hall and were not up for any awards. We all knew what was going on. She was there for room searches. Room searches were when all the guys on the hall would wait in the common room while, one by one, each went into their rooms with a dean who turned the room upside down looking for contraband. Mather had no regard for privacy or the constitution. It was its own world with its own rules. How the hell could they do this three weeks before graduation? I was smart enough to hide my weed stash in the basement, but I did have one water bottle filled with vodka in my refrigerator. That would be enough to destroy me.

My stomach pushed up to the base of my throat. Clementeen was good. I remembered her last raid and the witch finding a glass pipe in my friend's shoe bag. Thorough was an understatement. I tapped my nails on a chair and thought of ways that I could get it out of there. My only chance was to ask if I could grab my homework and casually grab the bottle as I left. My floor master would have to come with me, though. It was too risky. I decided that my chances were better if I did nothing at all. My tapping increased, and some of the guys in the room looked at me with concern. Most of them were clients and had their futures at risk too. I gave them half nods to assure they would be okay. There were seven other water bottles in the refrigerator filled with actual water, and I doubted that she'd open and smell them all. Still, even if she only opened one, that gave me a 12.5 percent chance of getting fucked. I was just about ready to shit my pants as my turn came along.

After what seemed like an eternity, Ms. Clementeen asked me to stand up and accompany her into my room.

"Okay, Callum, you know how this works." By that time of the year, room searches had become a regular event in Buchannan. "Now, is there anything you want to show or tell me before I take a look around?" she asked.

"No." I said.

As she looked around, I prayed to God that she wouldn't find the bottle. This could knock me off the path.

Lord, please help me out here. I am so sorry for anything bad that I've done. I promise I'll be better. Anything you want. Please God.

I needed to get off clean. I knew that my father would disown me if I got kicked out of Mather and lost my way into Penn. Ms. Clementeen obviously thought that I was hiding something because she was searching as if she'd lost a diamond. She made me strip my bed and flip over my mattress for her. She tore through all of my drawers and dismantled both of my stereo speakers. The woman even poured out an entire bottle of Flintstones kids' growing pills (can't blame me for trying), probably looking for Ritalin or ecstasy. I have to admit that I thought that was pretty funny. She was really improving at this detective stuff. My smile quickly vanished, though, when I saw her looking at my fridge. My tongue went dry, and I could feel myself shiver as she approached.

"I don't think you are supposed to have one of these, now are you, Callum?" she asked as she opened the door. Refrigerators were not allowed in dorm rooms at Mather, but almost everybody had one anyway.

"I have a note from my doctor for it, Ms. Clementeen," I said, "It's for my acne medication." This was crap considering my prepubescent face could hardly push out a single pimple, but it made for a valid excuse. Doctors will write prescriptions for anything. Especially my mother's.

"I see, I'll confirm that with the health center." She grabbed one of the water bottles. She took a sniff and was about to reach for another when a loud yell came from the hallway. She put the bottle back and stormed into the common room.

"Keep it down boys, this is not a joke!" she scolded. Two

juniors had challenged two seniors on the hall to a wrestling match, and it quickly turned into an all-out brawl. The hall silenced as soon as she snarled, but I heard a roar of laughter while Ms. Clementeen and I walked back to my room. One of the guys who had already had his room searched was now parading around in nothing but a tube sock. She didn't acknowledge him. Luckily, she had forgotten about the fridge. I was off the hook. I thanked God in my head over and over as she looked through my jacket pockets. Just as I thought the search was over, she asked me for one more thing.

"Callum, do you mind if I take a look through your wallet?"

Shit, I thought. She was going to bust me for my fake ID. Well, at least I was pretty sure that I could not be kicked out for that.

"Umm . . . Sure, Ms. Clementeen. Here you go," I said, as I handed it over.

"My, you certainly have been doing well for yourself," she said as she skimmed through the wad of cash inside the old black leather case. "But we are going to have to do something about this," she said, as she pulled out my fake Maryland driver's license.

I had no response but low eyes and a guilty smile. Twelve work hours in the dining hall. No big deal. Could have been worse. Then, just as I began to exhale, she pulled a folded sheet of paper from my wallet that I was positive I had removed days ago.

Fuck.

The balance sheet. My heart sank. It was the list of names of my clients, how much pot they had ordered, and how much money they owed me. The list that changed my life.

"Is this what I think it is, Callum?"

Of course it was. The evidence could not get much harder. I was speechless. There was no excuse. I could not think of shit. People were creative. Guys had gotten out of drinking in a locked room by saying that they were gay and needed privacy. Could I say that it was just a joke? No. No chance. There was no way out of this one. I wrote *everything* down. Unless she believed that "pot" was code for "food in town," I was finished at Mather.

I remained silent while she lectured me and fought back tears. After what felt like an hour, she left the room. I locked the door behind her and punched it. It was all over. I was fucked.

11

EXPULSION

I WAS SO FUCKING screwed. I blew it, big time. No Mather diploma, no college, no graduate school, no job, no money, no wife, no family. Nothing. At the time, I felt like I had ruined my future. I fell off the path. The fucking path! I felt as if I had nothing to live for. Some of the guys banged on the door to see what happened, but I really didn't want to talk to anyone about it. They'd soon find out the hard way, as most of their names were on the list. I called Michelle and told her the news with hopes for sympathy.

"Are you kiiiidding me, Cal?" she squealed furious.

"I don't need this. Come on, Michelle."

"You idiot! Do you know what this means? I can't *fuck*-ing believe you!" Some mid-western new-junior baseball player would never put her through this.

I lay above the covers that night and just stared at the crack in the ceiling. My bedside clock ticked louder and louder, taunting me. A mosquito flirted with my earlobe. As I heard the buzz approach for a seventh time, I smashed the insect violently against my temple. I didn't feel anything.

I woke up the next morning hoping that it was all a dream. I looked in the mirror and the remnants of the bug's blood told me that it wasn't. I went to class. Lunch. Pretending the Mather rumor mill was not already in the works. I feared running into my friends on the list. Had they already been approached, or would Mather get rid of me first? Everyone knew. Assholes.

I went to check my mail after lunch, not necessarily expecting anything, but I needed to fill my free period. My box was as inconveniently low as it could possibly be, so I had to get down into a catcher's squat to open it. I started twisting in my combination, 12–43–then CRACK!

I felt a sharp pain under my left eye as my face slammed against the small brass knob of my mailbox. Six feet, three inches, and two hundred and twenty-five pounds of Frank Flaherty looked down on me with rage. He was an ox.

"Littlefield, you spoiled little fuck. You know how much you just fucked us? Who the fuck keeps a list?!" he shouted as he kicked me in the ribs. I curled like a dog. Nearby students stared. Still down from the punch, with no intention of getting up for the creep, I apathetically told him to fuck off.

I never liked Flaherty. We were in the same group of friends, but I had nothing in common with the double repeat hockey puck.

"Fuck . . . Off?" he slowly questioned. "Your wicked-smart idea of keeping a list might just cost me my scholarship to Colgate, you little dumb fuck. You fucked *all* of us."

The mailroom was silent. My face was steaming. I felt my tears mixing with the blood tripping down my cheek, and I just didn't care anymore.

"Does it *LOOK* like I give a shit?!" I screamed, like an attacking bobcat. "Get the *FUCK* out of my face *Southie!*"

Flaherty didn't say a word but picked me up by the shirt and slammed his brick fist into my right eye twice, dropped me like a rag doll, and stormed off grumbling to himself. It stung like a bitch, and I could barely see, but I wanted to tell him off again.

I got up slowly and painfully walked out of the building with my head down. Just when I thought that it could not get any worse, I walked into my room and saw exactly what I had been dreading: the blinking light on my phone. The message could only be from two people. I put my bag down, went over to the mirror, and took a long look at my stretched shirt and mangled face. My forehead pulsed as I pressed my puffed eyelid in and out, in and out, testing my pain threshold until it began to bleed again. Shit. My face was swelling quickly, and my neck and shirt were covered in blood. I sat on my bed still touching my face and picked up the phone. The first message was from my mother. She was crying so much she was inaudible. Serious, wet sobs. Like a dying animal.

"OEEEEERRRRRRR. Callum . . ." she wept in her melancholic voice. "This is your mother. Drugs? Really? This late in the game. Of all the *stupid* things I could have imagined, this just really takes the cake. I'm speechless. What are you thinking? Please call me."

That's basically all I could make out, but I was pretty sure she also said some crap about counseling. Nobody was going to buy that one. She was on something. Klonopin? Vicodin? Who knew. In her next message she spoke in a slow, cold voice.

"Callum. I am honestly in disbelief. This is an embarrassment. I could just give up."

I could tell the next few messages were also from her, as I could hear her unstable breathing in the first two, even though there were no words. The last one was a silence followed by a hard, uncoordinated slam of the phone down on the receiver, just missing the button for the click. Great. My own mother was ready to quit on me.

The next message was from the wicked witch herself, Clementeen. "Callum," she said. "I just spoke to your parents. You should have called them. I told you to call them. They are very upset. Please come to the Dickenson Library this evening at eight o'clock, and we will discuss your situation with the disciplinary committee." Wow. She was so full of shit. I could not believe it. "Discuss my situation?" Who was she kidding? There was nothing to discuss.

The last message was by far the most feared. It was from my father. I bit my lip and closed my eyes as the message played.

"Callum, you are going to be expelled from Mather. You dug your grave, and I can't do anything for you now. A resignation looks a whole lot better on a record than an expulsion. I recommend—no, I demand—you to go to the Main School Building and immediately resign from Mather. I'm sending Sergio to pick you up at 8:00 AM tomorrow. We'll discuss all of this as well your punishment when you return." Exhale.

That was my dad. No drama and all business. I kind of liked it. I appreciated how straight up he was, but I could also tell he was disgusted. He took the emotion out of my predicament. I now knew what I had to do, but the fact that I was leaving Mather hadn't really even hit me. It all felt surreal.

I looked at my trunk, an old box decorated with stickers of every camp or school I had ever attended and teams for which I had rooted. One last town car from Mather to Manhattan. My clothes were already perfectly folded in their drawers, so packing was easy. I carved my name into the top drawer of my desk, just for shits, but left everything else as it was. I didn't need any of this crap anymore. My walls were covered in sports and alcohol posters, none for which I especially cared. I took everything else I needed and tacked a sheet of paper on the outside of my door that read "For the Vultures." Someone would want my stuff.

The next twenty-four hours were kind of a blur. I withdrew from Mather by handing Mr. Ponzer a letter and shaking his hand. He had no parting words of wisdom for me, save an earnest "Good luck Callum." I walked out of the Main School Building and stepped out onto the senior grass. There was a lawn outside the Main School Building where only seniors were allowed to walk. All other students had to circumvent the sprawling lawn to get to their classes, no matter how out of the way it was.

"Senior grass! What are you . . ." I turned around to see Charlie Bailey, a black classmate from Westchester I never got to know very well, about to lecture me.

"Oh. Sorry man. Didn't see it was you."

I thought better not to draw any more attention to myself, so I went back to the dorm and tried to say good-bye to my friends. After Thomas, Branson, and Curtis either shut their doors on me or refused eye contact, I realized that most considered my list as an act of betrayal. I had ruined their lives, too. Whatever. I didn't think I would even miss them. The only person I sort of wanted to see was Michelle, and I wasn't going to approach her until she apologized. I knew she'd never do that, so it was really my decision to end the relationship. That was the end of Mather for me.

12

HOME

MY LIFE WAS OVER. I was fucked. Paul Simon tried to cheer me up in the backseat of the town car on the way home, but I was scared and alone. I thought of plan Bs. Diploma from a second-rate high school. Go to a second-rate college. Banks don't recruit from those. I could not go to business school without a bank job from college. How would I get a job? Could I go to law or med school? Was I smart enough? How would I succeed? Could I not provide a nice life for a family? Who would marry me? Eighteen and a failure. What had I done? How would I get back on track? I needed a Mather diploma. I needed my Dad to convince Penn to keep me. I started crying as we crossed into Connecticut. Sergio kept a straight face. I'm sure his children would never get into this kind of crap. I was such an idiot. I banged my head against the window and balled myself into a numb trance. Next thing I knew, I was pulling off the FDR drive and climbing up Carnegie Hill. I was home.

We lived in a five-story brownstone on the Upper East Side. An ideal New York childhood location. I went to Saint Sebastian's School, two blocks away, which made me the first boy in my class allowed to walk to school alone. The location became better with age. Around sixth grade I realized how nice it was to have three private girl schools within a two-block radius. You could not take five steps outside without walking through a sea of girls passing as women. Whether it was hiking their uniform skirts up to ungodly heights, spending five hundred dollars on sunglasses and thousands on clothing, dating older men, or blowing their study drugs, these girls did it all. For years, our house was constantly packed with prepubescent males pressed against the windows. Once we hit puberty, our housekeeper literally had to wipe off the face grease from the glass.

I stopped having friends over to the house after the fall of eighth grade, though. It was about six o'clock on a Friday evening, and I walked home with Trip Crampton. We had just seen a movie on 86th Street, and Trip was going to sleep over. I ran into the entrance bathroom when we got home, talking to Trip while I peed.

"Trip—that movie was insane! How could that girl die? She was so hot!"

"Uhh Callum?"

"Yeah?"

"I think you should get out here."

"Relax! I'm pissing!"

I jumped out of the bathroom and ran up to Trip trying to body check him into the doorway.

"BEUKABOOM with the HIT!"

"Callum, not now." He pushed me off of him and pointed

at my mother lying face down on the settee between the front hall and the steps. She was wearing a nightgown that had ridden so far up her leg, he could almost see her ass.

"Stop looking! Get out of here!" I pushed Trip away and grabbed my mom by the shoulders. Her long blonde hair was in knots and fell over the round throw pillows.

"What is it? What is it?" my mother blurted through the pillows. "Go to your room. How dare you?!" Trip was still watching.

I called Julia, and none of us ever spoke about the incident again.

I opened the door to that same entrance and inhaled the clean, familiar smell of home. My mother had someone constantly cleaning and disinfecting every item in the house, which evoked a sanitary feeling. I put my bags in the entrance hall and walked into the kitchen. There was a crystal tumbler in the sink, and an empty prescription bottle of Zoloft lay open by the phone on the desk. The house was silent. I could hear opera singing from our crazy neighbor's record player next door and school children laughing from the street, but the house felt like a museum. I looked at a portrait of my mother above the fireplace mantel and noted her familiar, distant glare. Never really in the moment. Always looking for the next happening. A trip, or a party, never life at home. I assumed she was at the Colony Club for the afternoon in efforts to avoid our first confrontation. Lord knows what she and her friends did all day: Bridge? Tea? At least she was up and out of the house.

I decided to leave my luggage and go back outside. I didn't want to deal with my mother's return or her "dreadful migraines" just yet, so I drifted around the block a few times, crossing streets for no particular reasons, and trying to enjoy my last couple of moments of lonely privacy before she returned.

It was warm, and spring was quickly progressing into summer. Two schoolboys that looked about seven were selling lemonade for fifty cents a cup in front of their pre-war co-op. Their white-gloved doorman stood beside them. As I walked down Madison, I noticed yet *another* French infant clothing boutique. They were going at a shop a block these days. I passed Mimi's Pizza. Its powerful aroma shot me back to moments sitting on the stoop with the guys and paying off James, the local bum, to go and scare the crap out of girls by giving them hugs and getting his filth all over them. James would do anything for cash. These childish pranks quickly progressed into him buying us beer.

I made a left at the Jackson Hole diner, where I used to take girls on breakfast dates before school, when I heard it.

"Yo, C! C, get ova hear you ugly mother fucka!"

The eloquence of those words could not be mistaken for anyone but James himself. I turned around, and there he was. Dressed in his Saint Sebastian's School warm-up pants and a Chapin School Volleyball T-shirt, the skinny, black, toothless man wobbled across the street with his hand stretched out for cash. James had Carnegie Hill wrapped around his pinky finger. He called it his "turf" and didn't allow any other homeless men in the area without a good fight for it. Parents would give him fifty-dollar bills for claiming to protect their children from muggers, and children would give him twenties for buying them beer. Private Upper East Side schools even donated old athletic clothes to him. He was the local charity case and had been ever since I could remember. I could almost swear he had a two-bedroom apartment in Westchester and commuted to work every day. I could just see him putting on his "bum uniform" in the morning, getting ready for another day at the office. His latest trick was to make up stories to parents about seeing their children buying cigarettes or smoking pot, so that they would pay him money for his espionage. My mother, when she left the house, was one of the few dimwits who would believe his word over mine. My dad had the only voice of reason in these situations. Sure, James gave the area a little color, but I wasn't in the mood.

I tried walking past him, but he slapped me on the back and held out his hand. Time to pay the Carnegie Hill toll.

"James, whoah! I didn't even recognize you. How have you been?" I said as I reached for my wallet. I could not believe he touched me. I could smell it. He mumbled some crap about a girlfriend he had, and I fumbled through my wallet. I was out of singles and did not want to give him anything larger, but he just stood there peering into my wallet. I finally dropped a five-dollar bill into his open hand. Without a thank you, James let go of me, turned around, and limped back across the street yelling at some doctor.

Shaking hands with James was enough to get me home. I needed to disinfect. Luckily nobody was there yet. I washed up in the kitchen, climbed up the marble staircase, and locked myself in my room. About thirty minutes later, I heard the door shut and knew that my mother was back. She would see my bags, so I waited for the intercom. No word for about fifteen minutes, until I heard her voice on the speaker. A slow, drawn-out voice.

"Callum . . . Welcome home. Come downstairs."

She was refilling the pretzel bowl. We both avoided eye contact.

"You will not believe what I just did," she said, as she fumbled to seal the pretzel bag with her back still toward me. The prescription bottle was gone, and the glass was in the dishwasher.

"Hi, Mom."

"I decided to take the bus home up Madison. Yes, it may sound trivial, but it's really quite lovely, and your father suggested we begin doing such things, so take note. It moved very quickly, and the window shopping is divine, and—Your *face*!" she gasped. She had finally looked at me. "Now you're a fighter? Is that it? Wonderful. Just wonderful! Who did this to you?"

"Mom, it's fine." I tried to hug her, and she stepped back.

"What is happening to you, Callum? My baby." She grabbed my wrist. "I do *not* know what Grandmaman is going to say. She would have died if this ever happened to one of my brothers or me. No, I'll tell you what she would have done. She would have disowned us and made us live with the 'slaves' for a year. Rice and beans and work. No books, no parties. You're lucky you're not in the same boat, Callum. You would not have been able to handle her." She might have been exaggerating, but she was right. I drifted over and hugged her.

"I'm so sorry, Mom. I really screwed up."

I felt her tense muscles collapse, and she leaned her eyes into my shoulder.

My grandmother was pretty nuts and intense, but she had a stern aura about her. Maybe it was her intensity that never let my mom grow up. I never *really* saw this mean side of Grandmaman, though. Apparently she had some sort of anxiety spell when I was young that really changed her senses. She had suffered various illnesses that nobody diagnosed, but I never really worried. Every day, she plugged away at her garden. She planted flowers, picked vegetables, and spent the majority of her time weeding the property. This was a dependable reassurance that things were okay.

I had to be hard on myself for my mother's sake. If I didn't, then she would try and take the blame, make it all about her, and we would hear about it for months. Another headache. Another cloud. I couldn't do that to my family again.

"I'm sorry I let you down, Mom. You guys have done so much for me, and I blew it," I said, still holding her.

I really did mean that. I knew I had messed up. She started to cry.

"Callum, I'm just so worried about you. I have no idea what is going to happen. Where *will* you go?"

"I don't know, Mom. I'm so sorry."

She kissed my head and pushed me away.

"Go to your room until you father returns. We will speak further this evening."

I dropped my bags on the floor and lay on my bead staring up at the ceiling. My Ranger's banner hung on the wall across from me, and my lead toy solders lined the bookshelf by my bed. I moved a stuffed animal dog that was sticking into my neck and threw it toward the wastebasket by my desk.

My Dad called me into his office before dinner that night and had me sit down at his desk. His suit was still on, his collar was crisp, and his office smelled like the Racquet Club, a smooth blend of oak, cigars, aftershave, and leather. I felt childish in my wrinkled khakis and untucked shirt.

"Dad," I was afraid of the silence and wanted to speak first. "I have no excuse. I'm an idiot. I'm sorry. Let me put it on the table—I have no idea what to do."

"You're not to do anything, Callum. Not yet. You've done enough. I will not let you screw up your life anymore. You clearly cannot be responsible for yourself. Now, I don't want this to haunt you and this family for the rest of our lives, so I'm going to do everything in my power to get you a Mather diploma, but God damn it, you better know that you do not deserve it. You don't deserve any part of it."

I bit my lip coaxing myself to keep his gaze.

"Yes sir."

"Now get up to your room and try and think about where your life is going," he commanded in his serious yet reserved tone.

I sprinted up the stairs two steps at a time and took a long, cold shower. I couldn't think about my life. I was angry with him. I was angry with myself. I was angry at Michelle. I was angry I'd been so stupid and not thrown away that fucking list.

The rest of that week got marginally better. It wasn't fun, but I was able to avoid confrontation more than you would expect. Since I was ten, my mother generally stayed in bed until eleven, and if she had no big events that day, she would be back in her nightgown for a nap around four. Sometimes, during her bad spells, she would not get out of bed for days.

I could not stand facing my parents for extended periods. They not only lectured me about being expelled every chance that they got, but they also would not shut up about my mangled face.

"I think I might go up to Millbrook for a couple of days, if that would be all right with you," I mentioned to them one night at dinner. "I'd like to get out of the City and do some thinking."

"Absolutely not," said my father. "How could we trust you at this point? You think you can just run to the country and drink and smoke yourself away?"

"Easy, dear," my mother soothed him. "It was just an idea."

"Not a particularly good one. Out of the question. Besides, Millbrook is on the market. We don't need you scaring away buyers with that face."

"We're selling Millbrook?

"*I'm* selling it, Callum," responded my father. "There is no 'we' about it. This is a borrowed lifestyle you have. And yes. *I* am selling it. It does not get enough use, and it's time this family begins to scale back on a few things."

My mother looked down at her lap.

Meals continued for the next couple of weeks with cold awkward conversations. I kept to myself as much as possible, trying to avoid confrontation at all times. At one point I overheard my mother ask if they could just send me to the military. At least in the Middle East I would not hurt her precious reputation.

Surprisingly, hiding on the top floor turned out to be an ingenious plan. My parents began to think I was being so hard on myself that they sort of backed off and avoided the situation.

I knew this could not last forever. It was only the end of May, and they would have to take some action. I was expecting summer school, or a job at one of my uncle's portfolio construction companies, but what happened was far more interesting. Mom called me down to her bedroom one night after my dad came home and told me that my punishment was going to be to spend the summer with my grandmother and her "slaves" in Locust Valley. She lay in her bed in a bathrobe with a glass of malbec on her nightstand. She had taken off her ice mask and put on her most solemn face. I was a little taken aback, and before I even mentioned our old housekeeper, Miralva, and her mental state, she said, "Don't worry, Callum. The doctors said that your old nanny is fine, and she really just stays to herself for most of the time." I could tell that my mother was still worried about how Miralva's breakdown affected me. She knew that I still had bad dreams and seemed to feel genuinely upset about it.

She clearly took too much of the blame for that mess. I would be fine. I was an eighteen-year-old man. I was tough.

It was actually the best news I had heard in a while. Aside from Miralva, staying with Grandmaman would be a joke of a punishment. We got along swimmingly. I hadn't seen Grandmaman much since going off to Mather four years ago. Besides, my parents were going to be in South America and Europe for most of the summer, so I was at least away from them.

13

THE OCTOPUS

MISS VENEZUELA OF THE 1939 World's Fair, Stork Club habitué. Debutante of the year. My grandmother was always the belle of the ball. She used to spend hours telling me stories about her younger days, but I only knew glimpses of that Grandma-man.

Ever since Grandpapa died, she had secluded herself in her Long Island manor and immersed herself in her gardens. The grandmother that I had always known was the Octopus. My cousins and I had always called her the Octopus. She somehow had a million projects going on at once and managed to take care of all of them, so we assumed that she must have had multiple arms, one making fiberglass pots, another wallpapering her garage with New Yorker magazine covers, one raising live chickens, two in her garden, one for her vodka, one for her cigarette, and one for smacking us around when out of hand. Once she became too old to do everything herself, she just got her servants to do it for her. She always had at least four people working for her, and although she called them her "slaves" or her "lovers," she cared for them dearly. These employees were there to garden, cook, serve, and clean. They were all illegal immigrants, and we had no idea where she found them. Every time one left, Octopus would just pick up the phone, and soon enough she was paying the air or bus fare for a new Jose or Berta. She legitimately ran the Latino Underground Railroad to the Gold Coast of Long Island.

She used to have a very strict schedule. She'd arise every morning at eight-thirty, have her breakfast in bed, then put on her jeans, Keds, and polo shirt and set out for the current project. She would work or oversee labor all morning, stop for her regular lunch of black beans and rice, and set back to work. The clock striking five would remind her to stop. Back to the house she'd go, to put on her gown and pearls. Her gowns were custom made using all sorts of ornate prints on delicate fabrics. Her two vast walk-in closets captured every color of the rainbow, and they were always one of my favorite hiding spots as a child. I would sit there looking at all the colors and press the various textures to my face trying to find the softest one. I once used her fur coats as blankets. Some nights she would glimmer like her dining room chandelier and the next she would shock your eyes with an intense pink or electric green. Once dressed, she would retire to the porch to watch the sun set and drink her daily vitamin: vodka on the rocks with a splash of cranberry juice. From there, dinner or bed, depending on the evening.

Everything about the Octopus was sort of a contradiction. Mud, dirt, and paint found themselves smeared all over her old wrinkly hands. But one could only see the filth if his eyes could adjust to the glare of her two huge diamond rings. Sitting down for a meal at her house, my friends always felt intimidated by her silver goblets, lace table settings, starched white linen napkins, finger bowls, and bells to call the "slaves." The meal itself, however, was too lively to frighten anyone. The only awkward situation to arise was when one of my sister's friends thought that the finger bowls were soup and began drinking the water with a spoon. My mother and I both started laughing, but Grandmaman kicked our ankles under the table and followed suit with the "soup." She took pride in being a gracious hostess, and her home was constantly filled with guests. On any given Saturday lunch with the Octopus in her paint-splattered Pepsi apron and muddy blue jeans, you could find guests of different ages carrying on conversations in English, Spanish, Portuguese, French, and German, all of which she spoke fluently. Grandmaman refused to go into the City because she claimed that she could not handle the walking. That being said, she still walked a mile on her treadmill each morning and up and down a steep hill to her vegetable garden every afternoon.

I hadn't seen the Octopus in a few years, but my mother told me that she had had "another spell." Her treadmill wouldn't go over a mile an hour anymore, and she was trapped in the house, lacking the energy to tend to her gardens. I think my mother meant that she had a stroke, but it seemed that she wasn't even really sure. "You know she has various projects for you to work on." One more Octopus Summer.

Later that night, I went up to my room and began to think of how I would explain my resignation from Mather to Penn. I had grown more confident that I would still go to Penn. I mean, I had to: My father would die if I went anywhere else. This letter had to be a formality. I could either have completely avoided my misbehavior and said that Mather wasn't right for me, or fessed up and talked about how I learned from the experience. It was obvious I should be honest, but everything was too much. I did what I always do and started cleaning. It calms me. I clean and I organize. Everything has its place and everything is immaculate. My friends at Mather used to play tricks on me by coming in and moving everything ever so slightly. It drove me insane, as I'd spend hours getting everything back in its place. I think I was just born that way, but my mother thinks it traces back to Miralva.

14

VOODOO NIGHT

"THE DEVIL HAS YOUR mother!" she screams as saliva flies out of her mouth.

Another sleepless night after being awakened by nightmares. I'm ten years old, asleep in my bed. A soft hand caresses my forehead brushing the hair out of my eyes and running down my face. I feel the repeated stroking motion over and over, but I can't open my eyes. I roll my head and see her standing over me. Miralva looks down with a soft smile and crazed, wide eyes. I softly push her hand away, roll over. Hot tears roll down my face. She will not leave.

My mother called it Voodoo Night. It is Sunday evening, and my family and I return from a weekend in Millbrook. I am in the fifth grade. I jump out of the car, and my mother nags at me to do my homework before I turn on the TV. Of course Julia has already finished all of hers. My father juggles our weekend luggage out of the car and opens the front door. I walk in behind him and confront a giant red X painted through the portrait of my mother in the vestibule. Her eyes are gouged out on the canvas, and a vacant stare peers over the room. I look back to Mom for a reaction but face a familiar blank expression. My dad tells us to leave our knapsacks by the entrance and stay close together. We follow him into the kitchen. I hold my mom's skeletal hand and feel it tremble. The kitchen sink is surrounded by flickering candles and filled with copper pots, silver flatware, brass tools from the fireplace, and dozens of starched linen napkins, all doused with water and sprinkled with dry lentils, antique coins, modern change, hundreds of safety pins, and leftover Easter jellybeans. The candy has melted in the water and has bled colors all over the napkins. On the top of this arrangement is a carved Brazilian toy demon from my father's office. My parents don't speak to each other or say anything to us. We remain silent.

We enter the dining room in a single-file line. Every painting and mirror has been taken down and stacked on the table. There are crosses drawn in red Sharpie marker across the walls. The chairs have been slammed on their sides with splintered wood scattered. My father calls out Miralva's name as we walk up to the second floor, but there is no answer. The porcelain planters have been turned upside down, and the roots and dirt from palms and ficus trees lie over my mother's precious Aubusson rug. I am not even allowed to wear shoes on that rug. My eyes are drawn to more flickering candles on the shiny wood coffee table. They burn on either side of a heavy encyclopedia that has been left open to a page with serpent illustrations. I begin to cry.

The faucet in the bar has been jammed with dishrags, and water spits over more silverware, coins, my toy soldiers, my mother's makeup, more safety pins, lentils, Hershey's Kisses wrappers, and multi-colored pieces of fabric that have been ripped into confetti.

Torn-up baby pictures of Julia and me are soaked in water and scattered on the staircase alongside Brazilian prayers in miniscule handwriting. Intricate flower arrangements run up and down the hallways. Every last plant from the garden has been yanked from the soil and scattered around the house. I hear water running in the guest bathroom sink, walk in, and see that it is full of eyeglasses. Sun glasses, reading glasses, my Charlie Chaplin glasses with a funny mustache, our ski goggles. Water is overflowing onto the floor. Everything is coming undone. I run upstairs. My bedroom has a line of five candles in front of the doorway. I see piles of destroyed vanity products everywhere— face creams, hairbrushes, and mirrors—and ripped-up pieces of paper with prayers to unknown spirits and gods scattered on my bed. I run back downstairs.

Miralva is inside my mother's closet, going through racks of clothes. She is soaking wet, dressed in white, and making frantic rhythmic movements as she mumbles hymns over and over, shivering. I can see my mother try to speak, but she is shaking with anger and fear.

"What on *earth* are you doing?" my mother finally lets out in a voice that silences everything.

"The house needed to be cleansed. It *needs* to be cleansed. The spirits have spoken. The voices have spoken. Do not be hostile. Listen to their words for salvation . . ." she replies in a cold, trembling voice before running into the master bathtub. She curls up in a fetal position.

My father tells my sister and me to go and wait in her room

until we are called out. Julia tries to distract me from the noise, but nothing will mask the crying and screaming coming from downstairs. My parents speak to Miralva in the same tone that they speak to me when I'm out of line. Miralva sounds like a dying cat. My parents want to take Miralva to the hospital. She asks them to take her to her pastor in Harlem. Despite their efforts, Miralva keeps throwing herself, fully clothed, back into the bathtub. She finally follows them out of the house, soaking wet, shivering and humming.

The next day at school, I can't think about anything except Miralva. I know something is wrong. I want to be home. I feign illness and leave early. As I turn the corner of Madison, I see a large crowd around my house looking up to the top window. Miralva is standing on the fifth-story ledge, screaming for help and threatening to jump. Julia is on the sidewalk crying. She does not want me to see what might happen, so we hurry down the sidewalk. I look back and see Miralva leaning half of her body out the window. Her arms flail. She screams desperately at the crowd now watching her, and, for a brief moment, we make eye contact. She stops yelling and penetrates my eyes. I immediately burst into tears.

Julia and I return to the house an hour later and see two policemen drag a kicking and screaming Miralva into an ambulance as she points, reaches, and spits at my mother, accusing her of being possessed by Satan.

15

MIRALVA

"I GUESS GOOD HELP *is* hard to find," my father laughed into the phone a few weeks later.

Two months after the incident, Miralva came back from Metropolitan Hospital's psychiatric ward; my mom said she'd been diagnosed as suffering a psychotic break. She was a zombie, and nobody ever brought up the incident or knew what to do. We barely spoke anymore. She had been with me since I was born and was part of the family, yet I didn't know her. Not anymore. A few weeks after her release, she told my parents that she was hearing voices again and took the next flight back to Brazil. A month after that, she came back. Her father had died, and she was alone with no family or friends. I guess my parents felt responsible, so they flew her back and moved her out to my grandmother's home in Long Island. There, she could live in peace and maybe work with other people. The Octopus had always claimed she could cure anyone from anything, and she was never one to turn down extra staff.

Miralva was a short woman with processed blonde hair, fair, almost albino skin, and coarse hands from hours of manual labor. She was from a part of Brazil called Bahia, and she moved in with us before I could remember. We were inseparable. She took me to and from school, played with me in the afternoons, dressed me, bathed me, taught me to dance the lambada and sing songs of samba.

At the end of first grade, my parents told me that we would be leaving Brazil and moving to New York. To my delight, Mi was coming with us. Since Mi didn't know anybody in New York, she always had time to spend with me, even on her days off.

As time went by, I became more and more comfortable in New York, but the change was much more difficult for her. She never learned English, she barely left the house, and I don't remember her having any other friends. Our relationship deteriorated. I would rather watch TV or play video games than play with my nanny. I didn't need her attention all the time. I began to make many other friends, and before I knew it, Mi had gone from my best friend in the world to a guilt-tripping housekeeper. I felt bad that we were drifting apart, but I easily learned to ignore it.

The culture shock got the best of her. She could not sleep anymore, so she started taking sleeping pills at night. The drugs knocked her out during the day, so she equalized them with uppers taken from my mother's medicine cabinet. I could see Mi transform before my eyes from a caring, energetic woman into a volatile stranger.

Until recent events, I never even thought about Miralva anymore. I hadn't spoken to her since the day that she'd left eight years previous. She cut me out of her life, so I had tried to block her out of my memory. But, memories come back, and I was going to have to face them soon enough.

My psychiatrist told me that I should look at Miralva with a more mature perspective than one of a scared ten-year-old boy. He made me realize that she wasn't just a babysitter, and I wasn't the only person in her life. She grew up in the northeast of Brazil, where Candomblé, an Afro-Brazilian religion that often practices voodoo and the creation of shrines, was prominent. I researched this for a school project in seventh grade and learned that the syncretic religion originated in the sixteenth century, when African slaves were shipped to Brazil and forced to practice Catholicism. In order to continue their original form of worship, they gave Christian façades to aspects of their native religions and communicated in dance and drums rather than dictated prayer. The various Orixá spirits were coded with saint names, and the new Afro-Brazilian culture of northeastern Brazil soon emerged.

I realized that Miralva was sick, and it wasn't her fault, but I still had the nightmares, and we didn't see each other anymore. Until I heard about my upcoming move to the Octopus's home, everything was fine. We both purposely avoided each other the few times that I was in Long Island, and I think my mother actually instructed her to stay away from me. Sometimes I'd see her looking out her window at me; she gave me shivers, but it was over.

16

LONG ISLAND

THE NIGHT AFTER MY parents told me the news, I packed for Locust Valley and drafted a letter to smooth things over with Penn, which I emailed to my dad's secretary, Tory, to proofread and send. She was the best: She did my entire application to Penn in one weekend. Of course I wrote the essays, but she took care of most of the paperwork and made it look professional.

I walked into my parents' room the next morning to find my mother was having her breakfast in bed with a blue ice mask over her face.

"What are you watching, Mom?" I asked, glancing at the Florida real-estate infomercial on television.

"Oh I don't know, Callum." She took off her mask and dropped it on the floor. "Please be a dear and get me a fresh washcloth from the bathroom. Needles in my eyes again today. Excruciating. Just excruciating." I soaked a hand towel under the faucet and placed it over her face.

"I'm sorry, Mom."

"It's not your fault, darling."

"Well. I'm off. Talk to you soon." I started walking out of the room.

"Wait! Don't forget to call me once you get there." Without removing the towel from her face, she continued, "Also, Grand-maman needs you to stop at the Walmart on your way out there. Please pick up a new chain saw. You can use your Amex." I'd also pick up some flowers just for the extra touch.

I then walked into my dad's office where he was watching the news and shook his hand.

"Bye, Dad."

"Did you get your letter to Tory? I want to read it before it goes out."

"Yeah, I emailed it to her last night."

"Okay, Callum. We'll talk. You better hope this works."

"I *am* sorry, Dad."

"I know. Just doesn't seem to be enough right now, does it?"

As the garage attendant pulled my Jeep around, I couldn't help but smile. The '95 beaten-up kelly green Jeep Cherokee might have looked like a piece of crap to most people, but I loved it. My dad handed the car down to me about a year ago after he bought a Mexican parts company called AutoMex. He got the boys at one of his shops to soup the puppy up and had it shipped to New York in time for Christmas. Dad really went all out on the sucker, from the lights to the engine to the uphol-stery. By the end of the "fix up," the jeep still looked like a typi-cal suburban mobile from the outside, but on the inside, it had the power of a Thunderbird and the luxury of a Benz. I slipped the man a five and set off for the Tri Borough Bridge via Harlem. Doors locked past 99th Street. A grin on my face and Britney Spears on the radio, just loud enough for people to notice.

It was a clear day, and there was barely a car on the road. As I drove past Arthur Ashe Stadium, I remembered how much fun Julia and I had three summers ago when we got Dad's company seats to the U.S. Open. Endless days of spectating and drinking with her and her friends. I was just the little brother tagging along, but it felt like heaven. I loved picking up their language, hearing about what they thought was cool, and listening to their gossip. They seemed to know everything about everybody and their parents. I was in love with all of Julia's friends. I missed my sister. I didn't see her much anymore now that she'd moved down to D.C.

I passed the airport, and traffic got even lighter, so I really started to move. I wondered how quickly I could make it to Locust Valley. When my Dad and I used to go out there for early-morning hockey practices, we could make it in forty-five minutes. I could beat that if the road was as clear as it was at five in the morning. This was more fun, though. I turned up the radio because I could and opened the windows. The wind pushed me back against my seat and this made it seem even faster.

Left lane, zooming. Car in front of me. Brake lights. Red. Shit. You're in the fast lane. *Get fast.* I shifted into the middle and noticed that the right lane was wide open, so I shifted again and booked it. Wooh! I was flying. I saw a blonde in a red sedan behind me, so I put my arm out the window and let the wind take my hand for a ride. Exit 28N came before I knew it, and I pulled off.

I finally showed up to Grandmaman's and was relieved to arrive but also scared shitless about living with Miralva again. Driving has always made me tired, and I needed a nap. As I drove down the long driveway, I noticed that the normally manicured hedges were rough and overgrown. To get to the house, you first have to go down a winding road, through a long stretch of woods peppered by signs that grow increasingly more demanding: "Slow," said the first one, followed by "Slower!" and then, "Drive at 12 miles per hour EXACTLY!" The last couple of signs were my favorite. "Sit up straight," after one curve, "Eat your vegetables," after another. As I approached the house, the pine trees grew sparse, gradually giving way to once-meticulously tended gardens that surrounded the main house and drew you in different directions via stone paths to fountains, gazebos, a Japanese tea house, and a tennis court far off down the hill. The possibilities around these gardens were endless.

I immediately wanted go to my favorite spot, which was a white gazebo overlooking the water. I could sit there for hours on end, staring over the rose bushes at the tiny waves of the Long Island Sound slapping against the pebble beaches of the North Shore. That being said, I had to go say hi to Grandma-man first. After slowly passing by the gardens, I continued driving up the hill to the turn-of-the-century Georgian colonial. Its rough brick exterior contrasted beautifully with the property's once-precise gardens.

The colossal wooden front doors were closed, and the familiar "I'm in the jardin" sign wasn't hanging in its place. It must have been a rest day for the Octopus. As I walked through the door, I almost expected to see my Havishamish grandmother dancing away with some boy in the front hall. I could hear Spanish telenovelas from the TV in the kitchen. Her study was empty, so I went upstairs to her bedroom, and sure enough, there was the Octopus inching away on a treadmill with a cigarette in one hand and her cranberry vodka in the other. Her personal physiotherapy. She was happy to see me but was even happier to have another slave. Her face lit up upon my entrance, her eyes telling me effortlessly that it would be mere minutes before I was put work outside.

17

BACK TO WORK

GRANDMAMAN'S STRIDES ON the treadmill were deliberate and slow, and her once-porcelain face was wrinkled and strained. I could tell that she had changed. Her eyes wandered off as quickly as they lit up. My parents said she was suffering from high blood pressure, but I knew that the Octopus was physically unbreakable. I was more scared that she was showing signs of dementia or something.

"Hi, Grandmaman! It's wonderful to see you!"

"Yes, lovie," she responded in a frail and measured voice. "Come over and give me a hug, Mosquito." She had called me that ever since I was little. To her, crying infants resembled the pestering little bug. "I'm so pleased to have you here, Callum, despite why you were sent. Wait. Your eye." She pointed. "What happened?"

"Well, it's kind of a lo—"

"You probably deserved it, didn't you? Hah. You inherited my temper. We will have plenty of time to shape you up later. Right now, I need your muscle."

I felt very weak at that moment.

"Have you seen the cemetery? It is completely overgrown. Start there."

I began to walk off to place my bags in my room when she called out, "And don't you worry about you-know-who, Mosquito. She has been perfectly well behaved, and I have told her not to stray too far from the other 'slaves' wing while you're around."

Five minutes later I was in "the cemetery," digging weeds like a madman. This wasn't an authentic cemetery, but a rose garden and resting place of Humphrey, Chika, Fluffy, Pebbles, and Diana. I wondered if the Octopus would want to be buried there too. I was stationed between two South American giants. Thankfully, after a few years of Hispanic nannies, two summers studying in Spain, and a solid base in Portuguese, my Spanish was pretty good. At least good enough to get by with my two new coworkers.

Aurelio was a man in his midthirties who had just arrived from the mountains of Peru. He was only about five foot nine, but the guy was an ox. When I asked him how my grandmother was, he said that she was very moody, but that he had learned a lot from her and was making good money to send back to his family. I didn't even dare to ask what kind of semi-minimum wage she was paying him.

To the left of me, Miguel (or the Green Giant, as the Octopus called him) was reaping in on the benefits of his new intern. He had worked for Grandmaman for a few years and easily assumed his role as my new foreman. He sat his fat ass on a rock and told me what to do, laughing whenever I was too weak to push or pull something.

"Huy huy huy." He smiled as he used his John Deere T-shirt to wipe the sweat beads off of his fat face.

My hands were already raw, and I could feel the pressure of my left loafer digging into a blister on the side of my heel.

After I told Miguel why I was sent home from school, he would not shut up about me getting him drugs or sneaking him booze from my grandmother's bar. I should have had him fired right then and there. I was actually planning on it, until Aurelio showed me where they slept. The Octopus had transformed the old tractor shed into the men's quarters. The women slept in the "wing," which was really just the attic above the living room, which wasn't that bad, but this shed was filthy. Two mattresses with dirty Disney-patterned sheets lined the floor, and a black-and-white TV no larger than a record case was propped on a table at the end of the room next to a stand-up fan, which seemed to be stuck in one position. Empty beer cans were scattered across the floor. Most of the walls were made out of the old garage doors, and the room was covered with spider webs, pornographic magazine cutouts, and dust. These guys didn't have any air-conditioning and could only use the bathroom in the pool house, which barely ever worked. The contrast in lifestyle compared to that of "la Dona de la casa" was unbelievable. I felt pretty bad thinking about the queen bed I would be sleeping in that night, so I just shut up and worked in an attempt to prove that I wasn't a complete pussy.

The Long Island summer heat was sweltering and the humidity made my polo shirt stick to my back. I wanted to take it off but could only imagine what the Green Giant would say at the sight of my pale skinny body.

"Would you like some iced tea?" Miralva appeared out of nowhere, holding a tray with tea, ice, and three glasses.

"Oh. Hi, Miralva." I wasn't sure if I should hug her. It had been years since I'd seen her and more since we'd spoken.

"You should work here all the time!" smiled Miguel as he poured himself some tea. "We never get this!"

"Here you are, Callum." Miralva passed me a glass and put some extra mint from the tray into it. She remembered that I loved mint in my iced tea.

"Thanks, Miralva. I appreciate it." I tried to make eye contact but had trouble before she walked away. I felt guilty about my apprehension. I watched her walk back up the hill to the main house. She held the tray with both hands by her waist. Maybe it was all water under the bridge.

After what felt like endless gardening, I trudged back up to the house and collapsed on my bed. I did not know what to think about Miralva, so I tried not to. Minutes quickly turned into a few hours before I woke up to a tiny Ecuadorian woman named Berta poking her head into the room telling me that dinner was almost served. Great. Hunger aside, I didn't exactly want to make small talk with my grandmother about my mishaps while she inhaled the smoke from her Venezuelan cigarettes one after the other. Nonetheless, I hopped in the shower, dressed accordingly for an evening with the Octopus (dinner required a jacket), and walked down to the dining room. Besides the glimmer from the chandelier, the room was completely dark and empty. Instead, I found Grandmaman in the study, where she sat in a flowing green ball gown, drowning in strings of pearls. The television blasted, but I doubted she was really watching.

"I thought we'd eat in here so that we can watch the news,"

she said as I walked in the door. My mother had told me that in her weakened form, my grandmother had recently developed an addiction for the weather channel and local news to pass the time when she'd normally be in the gardens.

"The rain really puts me in a foul mood, so I need to prepare when it is coming."

I sat in the chair beside her.

"Now, Ian.

"Callum, Granmaman."

"What?"

"Callum, my name is Callum. Ian is your son. My uncle Ian."

"Oh, Mosquito, don't push me, okay? *You* are in no position." Her eyes doubled in size.

"I'm sorry."

"Now, your mother said that you are very distraught about this, but you don't even *look* upset. Think about all that your father has done for you."

I remained silent.

"He must be very disappointed. Don't you know that you have to grow up and be a man now? What do you think you're going to do with your life if you keep acting like this?"

The Octopus had given my cousins and me this speech for years now. It didn't matter if I spilled ice cream on my shirt or got kicked out of school, the speech remained the same. I kept eye contact, smiled, nodded, and said all the right things as I waited for it to end. She went through her motions but then gave her little lecture a new twist. I'm not sure if she had become more spiritual because of her "spell" or if she had just become desperate, but my grandmother actually made me come to her side, get on my knees, hold her hand, and pray to Christ that I was "not actually a delinquent." Her cold, wrinkled, arthritic hands felt alien. One finger shot out at a ninety-degree angle, and her fist curled into itself painfully. Her prayer went on, and she kept using the word "delinquent." *Delinquent. Delinquent. Delinquent.* I was desperate to go back upstairs.

"Please, Lord, don't let this baby be a delinquent."

It was embarrassing, and I felt like an idiot. There I was, holding hands with an old lady, begging God to make sure I was all right and not, in fact, a dimwit. Was she *that* worried? Did my family really think I was a moron? I tried to shrug it off and thanked her for her concern.

We proceeded to eat. The same story about a terrorist car bombing on the U.S. embassy in London played over and over again. I wondered if I'd go to war if I were ever drafted. I would've been such a shitty soldier. I don't think the army would even have wanted me. What could I add? Thank you notes? Firm hand-shakes? I would be useless to them. The way I saw it, I'd be much more valuable to the world if I stayed alive. Not that I had any idea what the hell I wanted to do with my life. So I guessed I wouldn't have fought. I would've probably gotten a gun and shot myself in the foot or something. No, I could never have done that. Maybe I'd just run off to some island and start a beach restaurant and live the life of a character in a Jimmy Buffet song or some-thing, marry some hot hippy chick with tangled blonde hair and tan skin and stick around there for a few years until the country forgave draft dodgers. Whatever.

I wolfed down my steak in about two seconds and stared at the TV, drifting off and wondering if this was the way the rest of my summer would go. At one point I thought that I saw Miralva walk past the door toward the kitchen. Those wide, white eyes again. Grandmaman noticed my discomfort.

"You might as well be a man and say hello. That was a long time ago, and you're going to be here all summer."

So Octopus hadn't sent the tea down for us earlier. That was Miralva on her own.

"Oh, I already saw her today." Grandmaman sensed my discomfort and reached for my hand. I noticed the sleeves of her ball gown were torn and faded at the wrist. I knew the Octopus was right, but it was hard. I should speak to her. I took a deep breath, stood up, and walked to the kitchen. Miralva was washing a plate as I entered, her back facing me. Her spine shot up as soon as I stepped through the threshold.

"Hi, Mi. How are you?" I noticed that she was back in her white uniform, which was normal, but it was the same white outfit she wore bringing me up, the same one in which I saw her in the bathtub, and the same one she wore on the window ledge.

"Thanks again for the tea today. That was delicious."

Miralva turned around and looked at me as if she was about to cry. It was really the first time I had acknowledged her since she left. She smiled softly and looked down at the floor as she said hello.

"It's been a while. You're bigger. You're becoming a man."

"Yeah. Thanks. I guess you have heard I am going to be living here for a while now."

"You're losing your accent. You're forgetting your Portuguese." I looked down. She was right: I hadn't been practicing. "How is everyone? Your mother? Is someone else living with you these days?"

I didn't want her to ask that.

"Yeah. We just have a cleaning lady upstairs. It's not like. Nothing has. I should go."

The conversation wasn't out of the ordinary. She was making an effort, but everything felt so tense, so forced. I turned around and started to walk away and heard her catch her breath above a silenced cry.

18

THE GIRDLE

"I HAVE HER ON VARIOUS sedatives, Mosquito," my grandmother assured me the next evening. "She has been very well behaved. I don't think she has mentioned any of those ghosts in years, darling."

"Well, good, I guess so. So, anything going on in the world today? How is the weather looking this weekend?"

I focused on the television. I needed something to avoid looking at my once-polished grandmother drooling out her chopped-up asparagus. I could not take it anymore.

"Do you need some help, Grandmaman?" I asked, motioning toward her chicken paillard.

"Oh, Mosquito, would you please?" Shit. I could not believe she actually said yes. She was too proud to have one of her servants feed her, but I guess she thought it would be sweet if her grandson helped.

I sat behind the Octopus and cut up her chicken into little pieces so that she could chew them easily, but she just stared at her plate.

"What's wrong, Grandmaman?" I asked.

"Oh, Ian—"

"CALLUM!" I interrupted her.

"Sorry, lovie. I'm so tired. Can't you just do it for me?"

"What?" I asked. "Feed you?"

She gave a sad nod, and I honestly didn't know what to do. I had gone from delinquent to guest to slave to nurse in the course of two days. Holden Caulfield to Florence Nightingale. This was pathetic. For forty-five minutes, I sat beside my old grandmother and fed her dinner, waiting about two minutes as she chewed between bites and wiping her mouth every time she began to drool. What had happened to her? She was the queen! As the last bite came around, I could not even express how happy I was about getting out of the smoky room that smelled of dead skin, cigarettes, and phlegm.

"Mosquito, could you do me one more favor?" she asked.

"What's that, Grandmaman?" I asked, feigning willingness.

"Could you go ask them to fix me some ice cream?"

No fucking way. Ice cream? As long as I'd known her, the Octopus had never indulged in sweets.

"Are you sure?" I said, as nicely as I could. She gave me a wide-eyed glare, and I conceded to feed her a scoop of mint chocolate chip.

"I'm really tired, so I think that I'm going to hit the sack," I said as I began to walk out of the room.

"Wait," she called. "I need one more thing. My girdle."

"Can't Berta or someone help you with that kind of stuff?" I asked. "Isn't that what they're here for?"

"Please, Mosquito. I don't want those hands on me if they don't have to be. Just come over here and help me up to bed."

I hesitantly agreed. I helped her up the steps and into her room, where she sat on the faded pink chaise lounge and waited to be undressed. I didn't even know what a girdle was. I just knew that it sounded gross and that I wanted nothing to do with it. Too bad it wasn't my choice. I lifted up her shirt and immediately looked away when I saw her old-lady beige panties hiked up five inches above her belly button. Avoiding the sight of it as much as I could, I slowly peeled off the Velcro straps to her girdle and slipped the contraption off of her body. As I took it off of her, though, a massive swell of pale, wrinkly skin came down at me from her chest. I honestly almost threw up.

"Phew. Thank you, baby. Now I can finally breathe."

"Sure thing, Grandmaman."

"Now help me to the bathroom." I was about to say not a chance, but as I looked at her worn-out, helpless face, something came over me, and I felt so bad I couldn't object. She sat on the toilet and took a piss as I buried my head in the cabinet above her sink, organizing medicine bottles and humming out loud just so that I would not have to hear or see the horror that was going on two feet to the right of me: spits of a steady whiz shooting like a broken automatic water gun rifle. When she was done, I helped her up and into her nightgown and brushed her teeth and hair for her. As I put the Octopus in bed and tucked her sheet in and around her, she grabbed my hand and squeezed it twice. The family code. I remember my mother telling me when I was young that one squeeze meant she was thinking of me and two meant she loved me. The Octopus then motioned for me to bend down, gave me a kiss on the cheek, and said thank you with the earnestness and innocence of a child. I actually felt pretty good about myself. I had not seen her smile such a lovely smile in a while.

Well, that's basically how it went for the next three weeks. Wake up, breakfast, upstairs, help Grandmaman out of bed and into her clothes, out to the gardens with Aurelio and Miguel, lunch with Grandmaman on the porch, back to gardening, dinner in front of the television, and putting her to bed. I would pass Miralva every once in a while, but we didn't speak. I could barely sleep knowing we were under the same roof, so I just read as much as I could. I felt sort of decent helping out the Octopus, but I was bored hell, and the more I helped my grandmother, the more helpless she became.

I admit it, I called Michelle every once in a while, but she never returned my phone calls. It could have been for a variety of reasons. I don't even know if I still had feelings for her. But I was bored and alone. That's why I didn't complain so much about the routine and my co-workers.

I began to get along with the servants more and more. They were helpful out in the fields and apparently got a huge kick out of my bitching and moaning over my troubles with the Octopus.

"*Mejor tu que yo!*" They would always laugh when I complained about the unholy process of undressing my old grandmother. Better me than them, huh? This was such bullshit. I was one of the "slaves," and I wasn't even getting paid. The only thing that separated us, other than my bedroom, was that I ate with Grandmaman instead of with the rest of the gang in the room off of the kitchen. I didn't really even like eating with her, but it was better than dining with Miralva. Grandmaman had changed. The old Octopus had a spark about her. I could see her fading. All she did was watch the news and boss her "slaves" around. I felt so bad sitting with her during meals as she incessantly rang her bell, making Marta or Berta come in and out just for a scolding about how the meat was overcooked or about how one of them served the vegetables from the wrong side of the table. I couldn't stand this for the rest of the summer. I was in desperate need of variety.

19

C.R.R.

CUM RAG RAPUCCIO. My one night out came about three weeks into my stint on the island, when I tried calling a girl from Manhasset that I was pretty sure had a crush on me back at Mather. Vanessa Rapuccio was not pretty, but she had a Mediterranean sex appeal that made up for it. Vanessa's family arrived from Italy a generation ago and developed much of the new real estate on the North Shore of Long Island. Some said her family was responsible for all of the generic housing complexes that replaced the Gold Coast's old estates. Everyone said they were mobsters. I didn't know. I just knew she was loaded and that her family was more fucked up than mine. Her parents, like many in affluent Manhattan suburbs, were notorious for their extracurricular activities.

My parents always used to joke about hating to go out to dinner in Long Island because they were afraid to see who was eating with whom. Vanessa's mom was supposedly sleeping with the same B-club tennis pro with whom Vanessa had lost her virginity five years earlier. Mr. Rapuccio, a loud, overweight, dark-haired man with a penchant for shiny suits and domestic cigars, had been slipping it to Patsy Studemeyer, one of Vanessa's friend's mothers for years. I once heard my father say that the Rapuccios were the kind of family that makes everyone else uncomfortable.

Vanessa was sweet but was a recognized slut. Her dark bangs over her overdone green eyes practically screamed for sex. She loved her "fuck me" eyes. She had given her first hand-job in the in the back of a sixth-grade-field-trip bus. By freshman year, she was known as CR for "cum rag." And yes, I was calling "Cum Rag Rapuccio." Pathetic. But I was bored out of my mind.

I tried calling her all afternoon to no avail. After my dinner, I decided to drive by the theater to see what movies were playing, but got a call back from Vanessa as I pulled out of the driveway. I could barely hear, but it was clear she was having a party. Perfect. A chance to meet some new people, have a good time, and maybe even get lucky. It was still nine thirty, which I thought was kind of early, and I didn't want to be the first one there, so I decided to drive around for a while.

Loops around Locust Valley and Glen Cove got boring quickly, so I got on 25A and took off for Manhasset a few towns away. Manhasset was supposedly where Fitzgerald resided when writing *The Great Gatsby*. Many famous early-century tycoons built their mansions there overlooking the Sound, but it had since been invaded by Rapuccio customers and strip malls. Estates were bought up and divided into generic McMansions. Like much of Long Island, its allure and glamour was replaced by shopping centers and auto dealers. Some areas, such as Vanessa's, were still very nice, but as my mother used to say, "that area of the coast is just gold plated."

Vanessa's place looked like it belonged in Monte Carlo. It didn't fit into the new or old Long Island. The pink stucco structure stood at the top of a hill at the end of a long, winding driveway lined with perfectly manicured cypress trees. Its façade was the size of half a city block. It even had a funny name on a gaudy sign by the entrance: The Lion's Den (after Mr. Rapuccio's mobster nickname and his love of his two Siamese cats). The place was awesome, sure, but not necessarily livable.

When I drove down the driveway, passed the house, and around the back to park the car, I noticed three Jeeps, a Volvo, and two Audis parked along the road. They all had boarding school stickers on them along with club and beach parking permits. The Locust Valley cavalry had arrived. I turned off my car and could hear music blasting from the basement. Relieved to know the party had started, so no awkward entrance would be necessary. The back door was open, and I followed the sounds of Journey. At the bottom of the steps I turned the corner just as a song ended, and the entire room seemed to look up at me at once. I recognized everyone's faces, and I'm sure they knew who I was, but no one made any sort of acknowledgement. Preppy manners at their finest.

It was the whole Tassel School posse. I knew all of these kids from the Club and spending summers going to day camp with them, but they had maintained a tight circle amongst the year-rounders and didn't really branch out to weekend and summer kids like me. Assholes. They could at least say "hello." I gave a half-ass sort of wave to the room, and the music finally came on again. Some of the guys and most of the girls gave me a head nod or an exaggerated wave, surely mocking mine, but they thankfully started to ignore me sure enough. The spotlight was off. I was about to turn to head back up the stairs when something hit me and knocked out all of my breath.

"CAAALUM!" Vanessa had jumped off three of the steps and onto my shoulders, screeching my name. Remember when I told you that Vanessa wasn't that hot? Well, that's mainly because she was a tank. I don't mean to say that she was fat because the whole world knew about her eating disorders, along with her other bag of problems, but she was simply heavy. Almost a miniature, more feminine version of her father's fire-hydrant torso. She had stocky, heavy Italian bones, which made her about five foot five and one hundred and sixty five pounds. The impact really fucked up my back, but I laughed it off with a big hug and a kiss.

"Hey, Vanessa! Thanks for having me. I was just stopping to say hi, but I think I'm going to—"

"Oh shut up, Callum! I haven't seen you since gradu—I haven't seen you in forever! You've got to stay!"

I conceded, and soon Vanessa and I were ripping into shots of vodka, which we chased with her father's '82 Château La Tour.

Her friend, Diana, joined us, and we decided to rejoin the party back in the basement.

"Oh, ping-pong!" yelled Diana as we turned the corner and saw the party gathered around a table. "I was named the Ping-Pong Princess at rehab last winter! I'll smoke any of you!"

To nobody's, save Diana's, surprise, there was no ping-pong. The crowd around the table was watching an intense game of Beirut. I really didn't get why people loved playing this drinking game so much. People at either end of a ping-pong table threw a revolting, dirty plastic ball into each other's cups to make their opponents chug. The cups were not washed and were recycled all night.

The ball was always covered in filth, and people were constantly putting their hands in the beer to retrieve the balls. I couldn't think of anything more unhygienic. It was also antisocial. Only four people could play it at once, so the rest of the party just stood around and watched. The girls never played, so it was always just guys talking shit to each other in an attempt to out-macho everyone else. It excluded everyone and was basically made for guys who didn't know how to dance or talk to girls. This game was the most exciting thing happening at this gathering.

Still, I quickly threw my societal judgments and hygienic concerns out the window as soon as Venessa asked me to play. I was only temporarily relieved, though, as Vanessa paired me with her friend Alfred, who pretended not to know me even though we were doubles partners for an entire summer when we were ten. Alfred turned around and punched the wall after I missed my second consecutive shot.

"Dude, just try and concentrate. OKAY?"

I nodded my head. Got it.

"Fag," coughed a fan, as I went through the motion of a practice shot. I missed again, and Alfred slammed both of his palms on the table,

"COME ON!"

I could not deal with this anymore. I couldn't laugh off my inadequate social standing at this party, so I started drinking on all of Alfred's turns to rebuild any sort of machismo I previously possessed.

I looked at the dirty hands of my partner and of my opponents as they gripped the ball, which continuously splashed into the cups I was now drinking. It was disgusting, but I couldn't say anything.

Thankfully the game ended quickly, and I walked upstairs past the living room, where a group of girls were cutting up lines of blow on a glass coffee table, and into the bathroom. I pulled the trigger to empty my stomach and felt ten times better because of it. After wiping the remnants of my vomit-splash off of the seat, I checked myself in the mirror and pulled it together. You're fine, Callum. You're better than this. I walked back into the living room and saw a girl lift her head up from the table, revealing a drop of blood streaming out of her nostril and pausing on her upper lip. She smiled and asked me if I wanted a line.

"I'm good," I said, as I motioned to her lip. She licked it off, trying to look cool. Sweet, I thought, *real* badass. I rolled my eyes.

I turned around and could hear the girls laughing at me. Fuck. Why was I acting too cool for this? I looked stupid.

"Actually, I'm kind of crashing. Mind if I take a bump?"

I bent down, took the rolled-up twenty dollar bill from the girl, tightened it, and blasted the biggest alligator tail left on the table. The powder shot up into my nose and dripped into the back of my throat. A strong cutting taste stuck to my esophagus, but my body was up and I felt a sharp little buzz.

"One more for the road?" I asked as I went down for another and bounced back up with a pop in my step. I licked my fingers and wiped the remnants of the table onto my gums. I was back.

As I floated back down, I saw Maura van Tinkle and a group of girls giggling by the basement entrance.

"Do you remember when we used to play "*Poor*" outside of the Morgan's?" asked the platinum tan van Tinkle, referring to the Morgan estate in Lattingtown.

"Oh my God! Yes!" cracked another girl as she got on her knees and pretended to beg. "Sir, may I trouble you for some change or any food?" The girls were in hysterics. I walked by, and Maura tapped me on the shoulder.

"May I trouble you for a few pence, kind sir? Please, sir?"

I pulled some change out of my pocket and dropped it in her beer. Maura looked at me in disbelief as the rest of her friends rolled on the floor in laughter.

I then started close-talking Alfred about how we used to play tennis together and how he had a great serve but that he was sort of a pusher when you came down to it. Obviously shocked by my new confident, blabbering attitude, Alfred warmed up to me, and we talked about nothing for a solid twenty minutes. It turned out that he got kicked out of Suffield his freshman year, then "resigned" from Avon, and was now finishing up school at Oyster Bay High.

"I might take a year off and travel a little."

I hated listening to him talk. He was boring and depressing. My teeth grinded, and I wanted to tell him more about *my* life. After telling him about Mather and Penn and even after I tried to relate about getting into trouble, it ended up being one of those awkward "Good to see *me*" kind conversations that you have when you run into acquaintances of the past who have grown into deadbeats. After exchanging numbers and promising to stay in touch and get together for tennis some time, I decided to give myself a tour of The Lion's Den.

Marble tiles covered the floor of almost every room in the house, and a giant fountain overcrowded the front hall. The walls were covered with Greek hunting scenes, the curtains had exotic patterns and Amalfi Coast scenery, and the house was everything you'd expect from the Rapuccios. I made my way upstairs and slowly walked down the hallway, as I studied every Rapuccio Christmas card they had sent out, from when Vanessa's older Sister, Maria, was born until this past winter. They all had straight dark hair and big bones and were all corpulent toddlers with large ears. The Italian Children of the Corn on steroids. It reminded me of a painting I saw in art history class of the inbred Spanish royal family. I then came to a door that bore a large pink sign saying "Princess Vanessa." I had to see this. I cracked open the door, expecting a pink paradise, only to see Vanessa, on her knees, holding the bedpost, eyes closed, sheets gripped in teeth, getting rammed from the rear by some guy I had never seen before. All I saw was her dark hair hanging and bouncing back and forth with their movements. I slammed the door shut and stared at the sign again. How regal, I chuckled to myself. It was time to get out of there.

I pulled out of the driveway and drove home on back roads at a steady fifteen miles per hour. I had heard various stories about the infamous Brookville and Locust Valley police pulling people over for drunk driving. My own uncle had his license revoked for getting caught bombing down Overlook Road after long nights of hearty drinking at the town's only bar, Buckram's.

When I finally pulled up behind the house, I noticed that all the lights but one were off. Actually, no lights were on, but there were candles on the mantle of an attic window. Miralva. I walked inside and thought that I heard a humming coming from upstairs. I poured myself a full glass of red wine from the bar, and then another, and made my way to my room as quietly as possible. There was definitely music coming from upstairs, and it was freaking me out. I crashed into my bed and buried myself under my pillows. I heard a knocking on my door about twenty minutes later but didn't acknowledge it. I wasn't ready for this crap again.

I didn't wake up until eleven forty-five the next morning. I felt pretty bad about missing work, so I moped into the kitchen for lunch, complaining about food poisoning and apologizing for not showing up in the gardens that morning. They knew that I was lying my ass off, but they didn't say anything. They couldn't.

To make matters worse, I overheard Berta telling Marta about how her seventeen-year-old son in Ecuador, whom she hadn't seen in nine years, had developed testicular cancer. He had had three surgeries in the past month and had both of his balls removed. No more testosterone, no more hard-ons, no more sex, no more chicks, no more sex, no chance of ever having a family. Wow. What the hell kind of asshole was I? There I was, sitting in my grandmother's mansion with a hell of a coke hangover, feeling sorry for myself because I had to do manual labor and was afraid of my old nanny, while this poor woman was working her ass off just to send money to feed her family back home. To make matters worse, I'd find out later that her husband had spent all the money she had been sending the family on booze and women. It was demoralizing. I was such a piece of shit.

What could I do about it, though? The only thing that made me feel better about myself was work. So for the next week, I was a complete machine.

20

RESTLESS

IT WAS MY JOB TO FIX the Octopus's abandoned tennis court. No matter how much I weeded that court, it seemed like the plants would grow twice the amount overnight. Towering branches cast shadows over both base lines, which helped keep the sun out of your eyes when serving but also provided a fresh batch of fallen leaves to sweep every morning. We dug up all the clay and resurfaced the court with fresh lines. As I dragged the roller under the hot summer sun, I cursed not switching to a hard court. I actually preferred playing on clay; I just didn't love the upkeep. My dad was going to love this. Callum the workhorse. I got up earlier than everyone. I worked the hardest. I even tried eating with the "slaves" / "lovers" sometimes when Miralva was out, but I felt bad for the Octopus. I was getting along with the staff, and I was feeling helpful, but it felt like the Octopus became needier by the day. The guilt from both sides was tearing me apart, and my next encounter with Miralva put me over the edge.

I was sitting in the living room because Grandmaman didn't entertain anymore and the space was forgotten by all but me. It was a spectacular space, with vaulted ceilings, a fireplace large enough to stand in, delicate green and gold fabric on all of the furniture, and pictures and paintings of ancestors and religious icons over the walls. It wasn't very well lit, but the privacy and mysterious allure of the place made it my favorite hiding spot.

It was about midnight, and I was reading a sad story by another Mather grad about the death of a camp counselor, when Miralva opened the carved, creaky wood doors and stepped into the room. I saw a familiar glaze over her eyes and immediately wanted to leave.

"Hi, Mi. How are you? I was actually just heading up to bed." I slapped my book shut and stood up.

"I just want to explain something to you, Callum," she said, in her voice even and emotionless.

"Okay, great. Let's talk about it tomorrow, though. I'm really exhausted." She looked down and then up again.

"Now," she said. Much more stern and direct now, almost angry.

I should have walked away. I was eighteen years old and she was nuts.

"Okay," I said, watching myself sitting down.

"Callum, that night at your house, when I did those things . . ."

"That was a long time ago. You were sick. Such a long time ago."

"I was *not* sick!" She snapped and then composed herself. "Stop. Just stop it . . . I need to tell you. I wasn't sick. I was fine. When you moved to New York, a dark cloud followed you. Someone cursed you through a glance. Your whole family was cursed. It was sent by the spirit of Exu who is and has been an indebted friend to Satan since the battle of good and evil."

"Miralva, please. I really have to go to bed." I started to get up, and she put her hand up on my shoulder and looked right through my eyes.

"You must understand my actions. Oxala is the Supreme Being, and Exu is his messenger to the mortals. He is a messenger of good and also of evil. Your curse led Exu to possess the house and to keep his evil eye to watch over you always. I needed to save you. Your parents had taken you away from your roots where you were safe and meant to flower. They left you vulnerable to the will of Exu. In Brazil, you were to blossom into a strong leader. Your parents took you away from the good in your life and left you exposed to the dark elements of Macumba spirits. I thought you would learn to protect yourself in school, but the Jesus they taught you about was weak. He simply danced around like a puppet, a toy or a doll. He didn't protect you. I could see you change. Every night I prayed for help and intervention. Finally, the spirits of Oxala and Yemanja, the Queen of the Seas, descended to me. They agreed to help but demanded offerings and a total cleansing of my surroundings. This was the only way I could protect you from Exu. It was their will. Callum, they *spoke* to me and told me how to save you and your family from yourselves and from Exu. I did it all for you."

I started to tear, unsure if I was furious or terrified. I pushed her arm away and ran up to my room, locking the door behind me. I had to get out of there.

A week passed, and I found myself either working or sitting by the Octopus's side at all times. I didn't even mention

Miralva's name. I didn't want to think about her. I pretended the whole thing didn't even happen. I didn't want to be responsible for sending her back into the nut house in a straight jacket. She had once been like a mother to me, and I could not do that to her, no matter how scary she had become.

At night, I began to search the Internet for alternative activities that would get me out of the house. There were cooking classes, sports teams, community service projects, anything. I knew my parents would be leaving for their trip soon. Time was of the essence. In order for my parents to agree, I'd have to find something that they considered productive. Something academic would be my best bet. I'd never been more excited about the idea of summer school before.

By then, I was a little over a month into my stay, and my parents came out for the weekend to say good-bye. They were going on an extended business trip up the coast of Brazil and then flying directly to London. It would be my last shot at convincing them to alter my sentencing.

In any case, Mom knew something was off.

"Are you sure you'll be okay, Callum?" she kept asking.

"Of course, Mom. You guys have fun!"

"I worry about you."

"I'll be fine. I'm doing well."

I didn't say anything about Miralva. Not like she could, or would, do anything. I was just happy to have them out of the country. The point was that I would not have them looking over my back for the next month and a half. This was the perfect opportunity to escape. Between Miralva, the "slaves," and the Octopus, there was no way I could stay in Locust Valley.

That Saturday before dinner, I walked into my mother's

bedroom, sat down on her ottoman, and handed her a printout about a creative writing class at NYU.

"What's this, honey?"

"It's a class I really want to sign up for, Mom. I'm getting a ton out of being here with Grandmaman, but I think it's important for me to continue some sort of academic program this summer, especially as my acceptance to Penn is under review."

"Well, where is it? When does it meet?"

"It's in the City, but it's only three days a week, and I can come in and out pretty easily."

"Let me think about it."

"Can you at least consider it? Talk to Dad for me?"

"We will think about it, Callum. Now let me get changed for dinner."

I had always enjoyed English at Mather but wasn't especially drawn to the course. I was more excited about an excuse to return to the City. My mom actually seemed to like the idea as well, but Dad knew that it was risky for me to be in town with school out for summer vacation. Too many distractions, too much free time, too much trouble.

After a couple of days of impeccable behavior and bullshitting about how I really enjoyed helping Grandmaman, my mother convinced Dad that I could drive in for three nights a week and take the class, as long as I was in Locust Valley helping for the rest of the time. I was saved.

21

FREEDOM

I DROVE INTO Manhattan that Tuesday with a fire inside of me and a shit-eating grin on my face. I was so pumped that I actually went to this creative writing workshop thing, just to check it out. Who knew? It could not have been that bad. Writing had always been my strong point in school, and it only met for three hours a day. I parked my car in front of an NYU dorm near Union Square. A trophy wife was having a cigarette on the corner while her husband helped her daughter move in for summer classes. I was feeling confident, and her curvy figure, accentuated by her tight khaki shorts and tiny orange T-shirt, begged me to approach her. I jogged across the street pretending that I was in a hurry and asked, "Excuse me, Miss, do you happen to know where the McAllister Writing House is? I'm a professor here for the summer, and I'm already late for my first class."

"Yeah right, kid," she said. "I think that maybe in a few years you could be old enough to enroll in a class here."

"That's funny," I said, trying to play it off. "I swear, one day my young looks will be a blessing. Can I bum a cig?"

She looked at me as if I were a meter maid and pulled a smoke out of her pack.

"Sure, kid. Just don't tell your mother."

Oh, fuck her. She didn't buy my act at all. I didn't care.

I turned around, slid the cigarette behind my ear, and made my way around the corner. I walked down the block, regrouping my confidence and new sense of freedom. Building number 132. There it was. I pushed through the revolving glass doors and noticed how the place looked like a half-ass office building. No resemblance to the structures I'd seen in countless other college brochures. Who would ever want to go to this dump? I took the elevator up to the fourth floor and found my classroom directly across the hall. As I walked in, I realized that I was already late. I spotted a desk in the back of the classroom and began to make my way over as the gypsy-like woman in the front of the classroom asked me, "And you are . . . ?"

The whole class looked at me, and I realized how lame the cigarette behind my ear must have looked. I pushed back my hair and grabbed the cigarette in one discreet motion.

"Oh, I'm sorry I'm late. I'm Callum Littlefield. " I snapped a glare across the room as I heard a tall, goofy loser with metrosexual square glasses chuckle at the sound of my last name. Little—Field. Like little fiddler, as in small penis. I'm short, to top it off. Ohhhhhhhhh . . . I get it, you fucking moron. I was surrounded by geniuses.

"Well, please have a seat, Callum. You have not missed anything yet," she said in a melodic voice. "You may call me Regina. Or just Gina, if you prefer."

She was wearing a bandana over greasy hair that reached down her back, a brown cotton sleeveless shirt that could have been homemade for all I knew, a navy sarong, and a pair of Birkenstock sandals.

I slouched down in my seat, pulled out my pen and notebook, and scanned the room for hotties. The class was mostly girls, only three guys. I did see someone that caught my interest, though, conveniently enough, sitting directly in front of me. I only saw her face for an instant because of the stupid classroom setup. It was a writing class. Why the hell were we not in a circle? She had dimples, which I love. I could see that she had a terrific figure. She had straight, jet-black hair down her back and wore tight, ripped jeans and a light blue T-shirt with some band called the Cheese Biscuits' logo on it. Not exactly my type, but what the hell. I was feeling good that day.

As the teacher reached up on the blackboard to write her name, I noticed the furry patch of hair under her armpits. Cute, I thought. Real cute. That wasn't what really got me, though.

"The Female Creative Mind in Writing," she wrote in huge, bold letters. My hand shot up.

"Umm . . . ma'am. I'm sorry. I thought that this was just a regular creative writing workshop—The Mind in Creative Writing or something? Isn't that what it said in the course catalogue?"

"Well, what is irregular about the *female* mind?" she retorted with a smirk.

"Nothing!" I said. "Of course not. I just didn't know exactly what the course would entail." What the hell did that mean?

"Okay, I *CONFESS*!" she let out in a dramatic voice. "You see, if I wrote the true title of the course down in the catalogue, then I don't think that any young men would sign up for the class, and then we would not get any difference of opinions, and then we would not learn from each other!"

"I see."

I knew where she was going, but it was still false advertisement. I should have left right then, but I wanted to see if I had a chance with the grungy chick in front of me.

For the next half hour we were supposed to write a short piece about why we thought the female mind delivered different creative tools than the male's. In efforts to cause a stir, I wrote a piece on the male mind and let the teacher compare it to the female one for herself . . . I went with something I had thought about in an exercise bike class I once took at Mather.

Spinning Thoughts of the Male Mind

I apathetically trudge up the steps after a long day of nothing. Why am I doing this? I should be nervous, but I'm really just too bored for the shakes. I look in the window and see fourteen little piggies lined up and ready for action. Don't even look at me. Ugghh. Shivers down my back. One whale saddles up to the right of me, and I think I might vomit. I would gladly give Shylock a pound of flesh from this beast, but I doubt anyone would want it. The fatty lumps around the bottom of her spandex lazily gaze at me, so I look ahead and begin to peddle. Peddle away from this monstrosity. Music is on. GooGoo Dolls, "Broadway is Dark Tonight." So are my thoughts. A spicy little anorexic minx gets on the other bike in front of me, tight blue tank top covering her washboard abs and peach shaped breasts. Her lacrosse shorts caress her nonexistent ass, and I think about the things I could do to her. She turns around and sees me staring at her panty lining and smiles. Those Angelina Jolie lips need to engulf me. I don't care about her lack of body. I just picture her up against a wall, and I love it.

I notice the instructor going at it, and we are well into the class. Different instructor than last week. I like her. Brown hair, plain face, large eyes, bigger tits, tight stomach, and nice . . . Wait, who am I kidding? Her ass is huge. So are her legs, but at least it's muscle. She reminds me of the lifeguard at the beach club who nobody can make up their mind about. I'd definitely fuck her. She's got the look.

I am exhausted. She is blasting techno music, and I fucking hate it. The other girl puts on motivational eighties music. This stuff is an axe across my left temple. I peddle harder.

"Allright, everyone, turn up the resistance, we're going up a hill."

Oh fuck. The fan is not even hitting me. Darkness and heat surround me. Her voice bothers me. The only illumination comes from a black light making everyone's skin look the same dark purple. I can feel sweat drip across my neck and stream down my chest into my belly button. Exhausted. My neck hurts, and my legs are cement. I don't know how they are moving anymore. I've lost control. I can only look six feet ahead of me at the glimmering, sweaty breasts of this whore of a drill sergeant. Fuck her, this humid cave, and every beast inside of it.

"Okay, we are getting there!!! And do you know what's at the top of the hill?"

"What?" I angrily mutter, wishing this bike would actually move so I could pounce her.

"Sprints and jumps, baby. Pump it up, you guys!"

She looks into my eyes as she says "pump" in her screeching voice.

"PUMP," her lips replay in slow motion. "Come on, you can go harder than that! WORK with me!"

She is going much faster than I am and is yelling at the top of her lungs for me to catch up, demanding my strength, questioning my manhood.

"Okay, now jumps, with the rhythm."

She turns up this horrible pop song by a girl you feel bad to look at, and I want to explode.

"One, two, one, two, one, two, up and down, you guys. Come on. Harder. With the music!"

I can't even think anymore. My body is working too hard for her. All I can do is follow instructions and try and please her. I peddle. I jump. Up, down. Up, down. Harder. Harder. Harder. Whatever she wants.

I look down at the bony ass in front of me, and I don't even think twice about it. She's nothing, kid's stuff. I want the queen of this pride.

"Come on, you guys!" she roars with less authority than her last cry.

Yes, I can tell she is out of breath now too. I'm getting to her.

"Five more jumps!" she pants. "Fiiive," peddle, peddle, peddle, "foooour," peddle, peddle, peddle, "threee,"

peddle, peddle, peddle, "two," peddle, peddle, and with a shriek, "onnnnnneeee."

Coast . . .

"UGH," I grunt and practically fall over my handlebars as my elbows give in.

"Now let it all out," she says in a motherly tone. Ew. Her appeal exits the room, along with her bitchy edge. "Now, cool off at your own cadence and stretch it out, guys."

I feel disgusting. I'm soaking with sweat. I can smell my own body odor and, even worse, the stench of sweaty cellulite around me. These people should be ashamed of themselves. The instructor smiles at me and says nice job.

"You can relax now."

It's like we're spooning, and I want to throw up. There's nothing worse than waking up with the fat chick.

Fuck you. The cool-off song is some horrible Sarah McLachlan ballad, and I can't take it anymore. I'm starving, I have to piss, and I'm late for dinner. I get off my bike and walk out of the room without washing my hands or my handlebars. I don't make eye contact, and I don't look back. I'll never see her again.

Slut.

I wonder who will teach the six fifteen tomorrow.

"Any brave souls who would like to share their pieces?" our teacher tempted the room.

A few eager hands shot up. Regina's eyes met mine, but I looked down cowardly without volunteering my paper. Maybe I didn't want to make any enemies yet.

Gabrielle: Black ponytail, pale, short, blue jeans, green T-shirt.

"*I'll get right to the point. Men are stupid and ignorant. Where I may use my imagination to create stories involving feelings, emotions, and complex situations, my male counterpart will use his mind to think of aliens, explosions, and grotesque fights.*"

Shiloh: Male, long dirty blonde hair, pink cheeks, skinny, tall, black jeans, remnants of acne, lipstick?

"*Men and women have the same mental tools. Our strengths and weaknesses are equal. Our experiences differentiate us. Can a girl put the true pain and humiliation into a story about a boy being picked on as a male can? Does she know the sensation of underwear ripping through her butt from a wedgie? Has she lost every game in gym class for her entire life? Has anyone ever purposely knocked her lunch tray out of her hands in front of a full cafeteria of other students?*"

Jeanne: Female linebacker, would absolutely crush me, black T-shirt, cargo pants, worker boots, absurd amount of string and hemp bracelets.

"*Men don't have creative minds, they have dicks. Dicks and balls. Their balls are their engines, and their dicks are their rudders. Everything has to do with sex. Ever notice how forced and out of place sex scenes are in novels? Are the guys masturbating as they write? I don't know. Why do they write in the first place? I'll tell you why. So they can get laid later.*"

Boy was I *glad* that I didn't have to share mine. Whoa. I'd have to tone it down in the future if I didn't want to be tarred and feathered by September. We were then told to pair up, so I quickly nabbed the class cutie before anybody else could. Shiloh was lost without a partner. He looked in our direction, fishing for an invitation, but I would not bite. Thank God our teacher finally called him over to her desk.

The pairs were for peer editing. We'd submit our final drafts before the next class. Good. No harm done today. Mine might have been a little coarse, but perhaps good for this situation. This little minion would think I'm a beast. Maybe.

"Cheese Biscuits, huh? I love those guys," I said as I pulled my chair around to her desk.

"Really?" she asked as she scanned my yellow pants and white polo shirt with glaring disapproval.

"I would not have picked you out as a fan if my life depended on it." Strike one.

"Haha. Sure, I have not made it to any of their shows in a while, but I got a great bootleg from their thing around New Years." I was good. "My name is Callum, by the way," I said as I reached my hand out to shake hers.

"Brenda," she replied, with a cold-fish handshake. "Nice meeting you, man." I smiled as I thought about how my mother would react if I brought her home for dinner.

"Where do you go to school?" she asked.

"Mather," I said proudly. This meant nothing to her, so I clarified that it was just a boarding school up in Massachusetts.

"I actually just got kicked out." Now I had an edge.

"What did you do wrong to be sent there in the first place?"

I didn't know where to begin. How could I explain to her that there was a difference between prep and military school and not come off as a snob?

"It's a long story."

I acted shy about my writing and said that I would prefer not to share it just yet. I said it was a little personal and apologized with a hesitant smile. She ate it up.

"I totally understand. I'm the same way with my poetry."

I read her paper, which was crap, told her how great it was, found out that she went to PS. I didn't give a fuck, and eventually I got her cell phone number and made plans to have dinner with her at Rouge 66 that evening.

PART 2

22

LAYLA

THE ZOO WAS GETTING louder. Women kicked their shoes to the sides of the dance floor and men left their jackets at their tables.

"Didn't I see you at Rouge last Thursday?" Mrs. Carson asked me, as we stood side by side watching others dance.

"I don't think so." Shit. "This is really a fantastic party. Thanks so much for—"

"And didn't your mother tell me that you're supposed to be in Locust Valley?" She dragged her vowels and smiled.

"Well, yes, I mean, no, you see, I'm taking this writ—"

"How is your mother?" she cut me off. "I hear she's not well." The fact that Mrs. Carson, who herself had been over-served and self-medicated to the point of notice, had the nerve to ask about my mother dug into me.

"Oh no. She is quite well, actually. She and my father are on a—"

"And *who* was that at your side, Callum? I'm sure your mother doesn't know about *that* one," she laughed. "Was she wearing a collar? That's terrible. I'm sorry, a choker? Is that what they call those things?" Seeing that I couldn't win, I shrugged my shoulders, smiled, and made my way back to the side of the dance floor.

Transparent, embarrassed, and ready to turn for home, I caught Layla glancing at me with a giggle. I didn't care if she was laughing at me. I was relevant. It was the most charming laugh I had ever encountered. I would wait until the next song for her. I built up my courage and was ready to make my way over when—

"Callum LITTLEfield?" A screwdriver of a voice dug into my eardrums. I turned around to see a beluga whale lurking over me.

"Hi there. How are you? Great to see you," I said as I stuck out my hand, having no idea who this creature was.

"You don't remember me, do you?" She sucked the air out of me with a bear hug.

"No no, of course I do. I've just had a lot to drink tonight, and I'm terrible with names . . ."

"It's okay. It's me, Mimi Pufton! I was two years ahead of you at Mather. Don't worry. Nobody recognizes me anymore. I used to be fat at Mather."

Who was she kidding? If this was her idea of a transformation then she must have been a legit cow back in high school. The name was vaguely familiar, but I still had no idea who she was.

"Yeah, wow. You look terrific! Well, I really gotta run. I'm being such a rude guest. Have not spent any time at my table at all," I said, as I began to turn around.

"Didn't you just spend the past twenty minutes making everyone else look bad on the dance floor?" came a soft voice from beside me. I turned around to two eyes critically piercing me, but they grew gentler under long lashes and a tender smile. They were the same eyes I had been trying to lock into all evening. It was her. It was Layla.

"Oh, hi Layla. I didn't even see you there," said Mimi. "Do you know my friend Callum Littlefield from Mather? Callum, this is my cousin Layla Semmering." I froze. A million words ran through my mind, but I could not open my mouth. Like a child trying to remember his lines in his fifth-grade play, I looked to my feet and searched for something.

"Hi," I said. That's it. Just, "Hi." What an idiot. I didn't even shake her hand. Good thing, too, because my sweaty palms were shivering in my pockets.

"Hi," she mocked with a wave.

"Yeah, I was dancing with my godsister Astrid a little bit. Or at least trying to, but I have not really hung out with her parents much."

"Haha. I was talking about your other partner! You two made quite the adorable couple, but you may be just a bit old for her," she said. "Or maybe you're into that sort of thing . . . ?"

I smiled and am afraid I might have also blushed.

"I was just being friendly. I actually fell and almost stepped on her earlier."

"Yeah, I saw that too. Smooth moves there. Hurting children? Well . . . I must say, I was getting a touch jealous," she said with a wrinkled brow.

"Can I show you some others?" I asked, praying that my hands weren't noticeably shaking.

"That'd be fun," she laughed, saying bye to Mimi as we started toward the dance floor.

"Bye, kids."

"Ahhhh, that was so embarrassing. Did not recognize your cousin at all. I hope she doesn't think I'm a dick," I confessed as we walked to the dance floor and waited for the next song.

"Hah. Really? I couldn't tell at all. You two seemed like you go way back."

I looked back at her corpulent cousin and drew another blank. "Not so much."

"Oh . . . Why am I dancing with you then?"

I froze. "What? Wait, no. I mean."

"I'm *kidding* Callum. Don't worry about it. Oh my God. I hate these parties. It's everyone I've ever met from preschool to squash camp. It's impossible to keep anyone's name straight!"

"Glad you understand. I thought I was the only one fumbling. Do you still remember mine?"

"Cowen . . . Minifield . . . ?"

"Very funny."

Layla was pleased with herself, and I was digging for something else to say.

"So are you going on the boat party after this thing?" I asked.

There was a planned after-party for the junior set on a "booze cruise" around New York Harbor. I admit, the idea sounded like it could be fun, but I had my doubts about being trapped for four hours. What if it was miserable? I didn't want to get stuck with a bunch of assholes. Layla changed the game.

"I don't know," she replied. "I'm pretty tired."

She didn't look it.

"Oh, come on, you don't even *look* tired. I promised my friend Collin I'd go. Don't leave me stranded."

"Collin Patterson?"

"Yep, you know him?"

"Weird, he is one of my good friends from Groton!"

Excellent. She knew that I had normal friends. "Then you're coming!" I gave her the same large, droopy-eyed look I used to give my mother when I wanted a new video game.

"I don't know. I have a tennis lesson in the morning and . . ."

"You're young. Come on! I won't know a soul!" That was a lie. I'd at least recognize most.

"Fiiiinnnne," she smiled. "Guess it is summer. No work to-morrow anyway!" She took a flute of champagne from an abnor-mally short waiter and swallowed it down in one fluid motion.

"You didn't put anything in that, did you?" she looked at the waiter with suspicion, and I could not tell if she was joking or not.

"No ma'am. I just poured it now."

"Okay, thank you." Layla looked at me. "Sorry! I'm just—I don't know. I get paranoid sometimes. You never know who is out there. I've had a bad experience."

I smiled with confusion and offered her my arm. We were attached for the rest of the evening. She was going to George-town next year and wanted to study sociology or art history.

"Or maybe I'll do pre-med. I don't know . . . I've always wanted to be a teacher or thought it would be great to work in some fabulous gallery or museum. Or maybe I can combine the two and teach art history? But I don't know, I think being a doc-tor would be so cool too, you know? Not a 'doctor' doctor, but like a psychiatrist, really see what everyone's twisted minds are thinking. Maybe kids? I work as a camp counselor at our church every summer and—I don't know. I'm babbling. Sorry."

We kept dancing and talking, and soon the party began to thin out. The drummer threw Layla the band's signature pink Lester Lannin bucket hat. It was the same hat the Octopus used for gardening, and I thought about the lack of evolution in preppy society. Layla wore the hat for rest of the night, despite how big it was on her. Her eyes peeked under the large flap, and it gave her a sense of innocence I still can't describe. While other girls put their hats down in fear of altering their hair, Layla relentlessly tried to impersonate Michael Jackson, flipping it on over and over again. She was a better dancer than I was, but she let me lead. Most apt female dancers try to lead and make me feel stupid, but she was completely graceful and put me in control. I could have danced forever with her, but unfortunately the band played its last song, and we had to rejoin the debauchery of young Manhattan society.

The cab dropped us off by Chelsea Piers, and we approached the boat warily. The ship was bouncing from the bass of obnoxiously loud rap music.

We looked at each other and could not help but laugh. When we got close to the boat I could see guys and girls, still in black tie, dancing like they just got off of MTV's *The Grind*. Arms were waving, roofs were raised, girls' legs were up on their partner's sides, or if flexible enough, shoulders, the Harlem Shake, even the Booty Bounce. It was nuts. Drunk, sweaty white preppy bodies in black tie acting like animals. A car pulled up behind us, and I saw Rob Patternack, my mother's best friend's dweeby son, get out of a white limo, fall to his knees, get back up, and stumble toward us.

"Littlefield! What's up, man? Have not seen you in forever."
He leaned closer. "Yo, do you have any blow?"

His breath smelled like a wet wool blazer. I remembered
when he used to lisp. We were not friends, ever. Maybe two
forced play dates. Maximum. He was covered in red wine stains.
Lips to shirt.

"No, Robert, I don't. Is that tie-dyed?" I pointed to his shirt.
Patternack shrugged it off.

"I've got some Ritalin if you guys want!" Ahh. I didn't want
Layla to think I was friends with this creep.

"We're good, dude."

Neither of us wanted to say anything else, so we continued
to walk down the dock, when I heard the projection and splat-
ter of vomit from above. It was Collin. A thick, brownish red
liquid ran down the white exterior of the boat and dripped into
the Hudson River.

"Oh no! Collin, are you okay?" Layla called with a smile.
She was trying to be nice but could not hold back her laugh.

Collin was always the first guy to either throw up or get in a
fight. Layla and I hurried on the deck to go help him out, but we
saw a large man, probably one of the boat chaperones, fireman-
carrying him toward the exit.

"Is he okay?" Layla asked

"Yep. He's lucky, he's my neighbor. I'll get him back uptown."

I probably should have offered to take him home, or at least
keep him company, but I flanged. I didn't want to end my night
with Layla. Collin would be cool. This was standard for him.

"Well, guess we should board, sailor," I said, as I motioned
to the vessel. I could tell that she didn't want to do this. She
looked revolted. Between the deafening music, thugged-out

dancing, and rancid smell of vomit, I wasn't crazy about this four-hour tour either, but it was my only chance to extend the evening.

"Callum, I'm really sorry, but I'm really just not feeling this. Would it be horrible if I took off?"

"Sure," I said, my voice only half filled with disappointment. "I completely understand. This isn't exactly my scene either. I'll drop you off."

We didn't talk much through the cab ride. The air conditioner was weak and the radio was low on 1010 Wins—"*You give us twenty-two minutes, we'll give you the world.*" The silent pauses were long and thick, until, halfway there, she blurted out:

"You know, my parents are in Southampton until tomorrow. Want to watch TV or something?" Pause. "I really hate being there alone."

Nothing could have made me happier. I tried to act relaxed. "Sure."

"I mean, don't get the wrong impression or any—"

"Shut up, Layla. Of course not. Totally fine."

I knew the invitation had no sexual connotations, but the mere fact that she asked me up set off fireworks.

23

GOODNIGHT

THERE WERE TWO FEET between us, and I moved across the backseat of the cab to sit closer to her.

"Hi there." Layla yawned and leaned her head against my shoulder. The front window blew warm summer air onto our tipsy, tired faces, and Layla drifted off the rest of the way home. We pulled up to a green awning across from Central Park. I paid the driver and nudged Layla's side. She was out cold. I watched the streetlight bathe her silk cheek in a yellow glow and leaned in to kiss her but immediately pulled myself back. I couldn't. No, not then, at least. It wasn't the right time. I watched her breathe and sleep until the cab driver asked me, "What da hell is going on?! Get out of cab. Curb side. Now!"

Should I carry her in? I opened the door for her and lightly rubbed her shoulder until she woke up.

"Hah. Whoops. Sorry about that," she yawned. "I'm totally out of it. Too much vino."

I smiled and reached for her hand. She let me help her out of the car but then pulled away. Was that a sign? Fuck. She definitely wasn't into me. No, it must have been my hands.

I don't know what my deal is, but to this day I believe my hands sweat way more than normal. My palms are constantly moist. In a movie, in class, at dinner, whatever. It's so annoying. At the time, I wished I were wearing gloves. Dancing school. Yes. Those little white gloves we always used to wear for ballroom dancing class. They were saviors. They protected me from nervous moments like this. Where were those little white gloves when I needed them?

We walked into the lobby and noticed the doorman asleep on his stool with a *New York Post* open on his lap. Her building had a marble-floored lobby with a huge floral centerpiece on a sturdy oak table. We got into the musky pre-war elevator and took it up to the penthouse. I placed my fingers through the cage and felt the wall slide below as the elevator climbed up. The formal living room overlooked the park and the Met. I pressed myself against the window to peer out at the West Side skyline, and Layla offered me a drink. I was going to go for a rum and coke to keep me up, but I saw her boiling water for tea.

"Whatever you're having," I said as I made my way to the couch in the TV room off of the kitchen.

"I'm making tea," she called "Hah. I'm such a granny."

"That sounds perfect."

I liked her apartment. It was spacious, but not too huge. Lots of family pictures.

"Please don't look at our Christmas cards! I don't know what my mom was thinking with those bowl cuts. So embarrassing."

"At least you guys look happy. My parents always had a professional photographer take our portraits. It took hours, and we always looked miserable in our cards."

"Why wouldn't we be happy? It's a Christmas card!" An unhappy picture seemed foreign to her.

She brought me a mug and told me she would be right back.

I took the chance to look around and check out the place a little more. I didn't even make it out of the living room, because I was so captivated by all of the pictures. Layla alone with her class uniform on, Layla buried in the sand as her older siblings crouch around her, Layla with her parents in one-piece neon ski outfits on top of the Rockies, Layla lying on a hammock holding her niece up in the air above her, Layla everywhere. My favorite one, besides some of the beach shots, was one with Layla wrestling a King Charles spaniel on a sprawling green lawn. Even rolling around on the grass with this animal, she looked composed, beautiful, and happy. That was it, though. She was so composed.

Layla came back in pajama pants and a Swiss semester T-shirt with a plate of cookies in her hands. She sat on the couch with regal posture, and I waited for her next words.

"Guess I'm the slob, huh?" She sheepishly looked at her pajamas. I had only untied my bowtie and removed a single stud.

"No way. You look awesome. I'm the guy who looks like a waiter." Layla's T-shirt was a touch too small for her, and I used every bit of will power in me to restrain my eyes from glaring at the soft cotton holding her breasts. I didn't think she was wearing a bra.

"Hah. It's very handsome, Cal." She offered me the cookies before changing her mind. "Wait. Let me microwave them first so the chocolate melts." I knew she wanted to go to bed. She hid it well because she was a gracious hostess.

"Thanks. These look great." I was actually starving, but more importantly, I was stumbling for what to do or say. "Want to put in a movie?" I asked. Good call, I thought. No imminent need to make conversation, but the door is wide open for witty commentary.

"Sure!" she said. She opened up a bookshelf filled with movies and picked out one called *Can't Buy Me Love.*

I vaguely remembered seeing it when I was a kid. It was about a poor, unpopular boy in high school that uses all his telescope money to pay a girl to pretend to be his girlfriend or something. Kind of lame, but probably sappy, which is what I was going for.

The movie started, and she sat down on the couch next to me, close enough to touch, but too far to put my arm around her. She leaned her head to the other side, which I took as a negative sign.

"These old movies look brand new on my dad's high-definition flat-screen."

"Cool," she replied. Why did I even say that? So lame.

"I'll probably pick one up for my room in Philadelphia. You know, actually I'll probably get a nice single since I'm a legacy and all. You know, they sometimes, kind of tend to hook us up." I couldn't stop. What was *wrong* with me?

"Well, that's nice." She wasn't even looking at me.

"Do you ever spend any time in Millbrook or Locust Valley?" A miserable dreaded case of verbal diarrhea. Verbal cholera. I was doomed.

"Nope." She yawned.

What to do? What do I do? Short breaths. I wanted to make a move. The movie played, but I could not concentrate at all. No witty commentary. Why wasn't she trying to return my conversation? What was she thinking? I was a moron. Was she thinking about me? Did she have any idea what was going through my mind? Did she care? Should I just say something? No. Do something? Don't be creepy. I laughed at the jokes she laughed at, two seconds later just to show that I was keeping up. I tried looking at her. Not looking, but really staring so that she could feel my eyes set on her and would turn so that our glances could connect. No luck. She was pretty into the movie. Forget it, I thought. Don't ruin a good thing. Don't make it awkward. You've had a good start. Don't fuck it up. But it was *so* good, and the opportunity was *so* perfect. Shit. I watched the movie, and the internal debate went on. Finally, as the movie came close to the end, I could hear her breath grow louder. She had drifted off to sleep. Great, Callum, opportunity lost.

It did not matter, though. I could have sat there and watched her sleep forever. Layla wasn't impressed with me. I knew this. But it was a marathon, not a sprint, and I felt a conviction. I would make this work if it killed me. The light from the screen gave her an angelic aura. She was perfect. I shifted over closer to her and rested my arm on her shoulder. The tiny hairs on the back of my hand stood rigidly. I was shaking. I sat dangerously close to her and began to run my fingers through her hair. The tips of my nails skated up and down the back of her neck. Was this nice or weird? What would she think if she woke up? Man, I was *dying* for her to wake up. If she would just roll over and kiss me, I could die a happy man. After a few moments, I grew tired myself and grabbed a cashmere throw blanket off of an ottoman to lay over her. I kissed her cheek, more tenderly than I expected to, and tucked the blanket around her.

"Good night, Layla," I whispered, now kissing her forehead. Well, I tried to kiss her forehead, but I ended up sort of banging my teeth into her scalp. She rolled over abruptly, and I jumped back to my spot, closed my eyes, and pretended to sleep. I moved to the other couch so I could lie down watching her and fought off slumber to extend my gazing time for a few moments. I kept this up for as long as I could, and then, just at the break of consciousness, I heard her giggle and say, "I'm really happy we met Callum. Thank you for being a gentleman. You don't have to say anything else."

24

BUSTED

"HEHEHEHEHEHE."

What the hell was that noise? Ugh. And that stench. I rolled my head over to the rear end of a fourteen-year-old golden retriever letting out gentle puffs of suffocating gas. There solved one problem, but the giggling went on. It was the kind of sharp, high laugh you'd expect from old-movie geishas. Sure enough, I looked across the room and there was a Filipina housekeeper giggling under her hand as I tried to put myself together.

I introduced myself and asked her where Layla was, but she just said, "Not here!" in a laundromat voice and gave me a note.

Hey Callum! I had an awesome time with you last night! We were quite the couple on the dance floor, wouldn't you say? I'm fighting off this hangover with a tennis lesson at the River Club, but help yourself to anything in the fridge. Call me later!
Layla

P.S. Don't eat all the cookies!

She was great. A few hours earlier I was idiotically trying to impress her with television sets and Ivy League legacy rights, and she just cared about dancing and cookies. I felt like hell and needed to hydrate. I entered a kitchen brightly lit by a huge bay window. It had an island in the center and an informal dining table by the windows. I opened the fridge and pulled out a pitcher of freshly squeezed orange juice. I drank one glass, poured another one, and leaned over the counter for support.

Though my hangover killed and my dinner jacket was a wrinkled mess, I didn't care. I just stood there, wishing that this were my life, that I lived in this apartment, with this annoying housekeeper, and this fat smelly dog, but more importantly, with this Layla. I unbuttoned another one of my studs.

Thinking more about Layla reminded me that she would probably come back soon and that I looked like a hotel bartender fired from his late shift. I decided to go to the bathroom to clean up a bit. I looked in the mirror: It was a rough sight. I washed my face, parted my hair with my overgrown fingernails, and took a deuce. There were a lot of family pictures on the wall. Mostly cliché shots of Layla, her siblings, and their cousins, but the one that caught my eye was one of a woman (Mrs. Semmering?) back in the sixties or seventies on a beach in the sexiest pose I have ever seen. She was wearing one of those old-fashioned James Bond girl bikinis that was conservative yet low cut, and she was reclining backward on the sand, letting a small wave completely engulf her. Her pose was strong, with her arms behind her and elbows locked for support. The way the water dripped down her cleavage and tanned stomach drove me wild. Next thing I knew, I had a chubby.

Great, Callum, I thought. Come on and get it together. What if Layla came home right then? I would have been screwed. I thought of brick walls, I thought of waiting in line, I thought of baseball, but I could not get the image of Mrs. Semmering sitting there, waiting to be taken by a wave, out of my mind. It was too much. I knew that the only way to get around this obstacle in my pants was to give it what it came up for. After about three or four minutes of hungover, exhausted masturbation, I heard elevator doors opening. Oh shit. It's Layla. She wasn't alone, though. I heard a man *and* a woman's voice. Who else could be there? I went flaccid and could not finish. My body calmed down quickly as all I could focus on was getting out of the bathroom.

I jumped up and went right for the door when I heard, "Laaayyla? Honey, you there?" It was her mother's voice.

"It smells like booze in here," said her dad.

FUCK. I peeped out the door and saw the sixty-something-year-old couple walk out of an L.L. Bean catalog and into the kitchen. Should I introduce myself? No, I can't. I thought they were away. I could have been polite and charming, but I couldn't get around the fact that I was a stranger in their house, alone, in black tie, looking like hell, and that my breath reeked of booze and hands smelt like dick. I bolted as soon as I heard footsteps of someone going upstairs calling for the housekeeper.

I made brief eye contact with a stunned Mr. Semmering as he peeped out from behind the refrigerator door. Without pausing, I leaped into the elevator and pressed the "door close" button at least a hundred times, pressing my back against a sidewall. It felt interminable. They finally closed, and I sprinted through the lobby, across Fifth, and into Central Park.

25

RECAP

"PLEASE DON'T LET ME have blown it, God. Don't let her parents have seen me."

I sat on a park bench with my face in my hands and tried to get my heart rate down from the near-disaster at Layla's. What would she think? I reached in my jacket pocket, pulled out her note, and smiled. I couldn't blow this.

I replayed the night in my head and wondered how Patterson was holding up. What a mess. I dialed once and got his voicemail. I called again and after the fourth ring, "Heeellooo," said a weak and hurt voice.

"OHHHH WHAT SHOULD WE DO WITH THE DRUNKEN SAILOR? WHAT SHOULD WE DO WITH THE DRUNKEN SAILOR? WHAT SHOULD WE DO WITH THE DRUNKEN SAILOR, EARLY IN THE MOOORNING?" I sang in a booming voice.

"Bro, shut the fuuuuuuuuuuuuck up. Please. I seriously feel like I've been hit by a truck," Collin whimpered.

"Collin. IN-credible performance last night, man. Barfing off of the boat? Pre-launch? You are an animal."

"Fuck you, dude . . ."

"Oh please, Patterson! Time of your life!

"I feel like death."

"Yeah, I'm pretty beat up too, but I had an awesome night."

"Guess I am going to have to hear about it right now, huh?"

"Haha. Yup."

I told him everything from the fat pig to running away from Layla's parents. I kept it vague, of course.

"So you slept with Semmering?! No way? Any finger blasting? You fuck her?"

"Shut up, Patterson. No. I'm not even having this conversation."

"That's such a yes. You STUD!"

"No. Get out of here. Good-bye."

"Bro, I heard she was fucking that laxer kid, Brooks, from Princeton. Dude is crazy aggressive with girls."

"Really?"

"Yeah—like he does not quit. Maybe just a rumor, though. No confirmation on them banging."

"Stop man. Whatever. I like her. Gotta run."

"Later, pimp."

The comment about Brooks was odd, but probably *was* just a rumor. I wouldn't let it bother me. I got up and was riding high and taking in the fresh air. Shirt unbuttoned, untied bowtie blowing behind me in the wind.

A cute blonde walked on the path ahead of me. White skirt, blue polo shirt, Jackie O sunglasses. I tried catching up to her, but she continued to speed up. Was she playing games? I squeezed Layla's note in my pocket again and realized that it didn't matter. I saw a different bench next to the weeping willow trees at the Meadow and turned in that direction to watch a little league baseball game. You could imagine the looks I was getting in my state and dress. One person even took a picture, but I didn't care. I bought a hot dog from a cart on the running path off of the field, sat back on the bench, and enjoyed the ball game. I was happy.

26

REMEMBRANCE OF
THINGS PAST

I HAD TO SUBMIT A SHORT story for the next day's class, and I had no idea what to write about. I couldn't believe I had to do homework over the summer. What crap. Whatever, I decided I should put some effort into this class and pass or else my parents would flip. Female perspective. Female perspective. I was clueless. I kept thinking about the kind of wild shit Miralva could come up with . . . the unregulated mind, the possessed soul . . . no, I couldn't go there.

I got home and decided to go through some of my late great aunt's journals that my mom kept in the linen closet. Weird, I know. It was a closet solely dedicated to mothballs, sheets, and belongings of the deceased. Might be something I could use in there, I thought. If I'm not going to be creative, what's the point in using my own efforts? I found one that wasn't half bad . . .

Remembrance of Things Past

Everybody has their story, and they are stuck with it. I was born during the time of the Charleston and grew up during the great depression, so I have had time to observe this little homily.

However, I didn't suffer, I was privileged. We had a house in town and a house in the country. I showed horses and won many trophies. I got up at four in the morning to go duck hunting with my father. We belonged to the Country Club, where I partied, tried Scotch and Soda with my friends, and learned to smoke at sixteen.

As I was progressing into my sixteenth year, one afternoon my father walked out into the garden and shot himself in the head. My mother, a grand lady from the Old South, who adored the latest fashions and European travel, was at that time drunk upstairs in bed.

This little habit had been coming over her slowly. She was now a confirmed alcoholic of the worst type. I say the worst type because there are violent alcoholics and happy alcoholics. She was a mundane alcoholic, who would never admit she was drinking. She would just stay in bed and announce that she was sick. The doctor was called to the house. He knew what the problem was, but came on numerous occasions—probably because it was during the depression, and he needed the fees. At this time, my sister, who was ten years older, was married, and my brother, who was five years older, was away at school, so I was the one who played hide and go seek for the bottle. I wouldn't bring any friends home for fear she might wander out.

Even before my father died, he had made attempts to cure her. She had made several visits to exclusive, expensive drying-out facilities in the vicinity.

After his death, his affluence also disappeared, and my jolly "friends" noticeably cooled or evaporated. I learned an interesting, hard lesson about the facts of life.

It was timeless. I pictured my mother in bed with a blank gaze at the television and empty antique pillboxes on her bedside table. My hippie teacher would find it even more interesting because she would think I was writing from the voice of an eighty something-year-old lady, but I kind of felt bad using it. I could think of something interesting on my own anyway. It would just take some more time.

I lay back on my bed and turned on the television. After scanning through the high sixties and back, I came across a story about four surfers dying in a car accident while driving to the Jersey shore. An idea popped into my head. It wasn't from a woman's point of view, but I rolled with it.

27

MOVING ON

DURING THE SUMMER after my senior year, the time in every boy's life when he joins a band, falls in love, or both, I grew up . . . the hard way.

My friends and I had planned the ultimate surfing safari up the coast of Brazil. We would land in São Paulo, rent a car, and chase waves all the way up to and through Bahia. It was going to be awesome.

We rented a 1976 Volkswagen van and strapped our boards to the orange metal roof. It was go time. As I spoke to the man at the rental desk, two of my buddies bought nugs off of a parking lot security guard. We then hit up the first pharmacy in site for valiums and beers. It was going to be one hell of a vacation.

A few hours into the trip we were high as a kite, two hours from the coast, and almost shaking with excitement. We passed by a few military checkpoints, stopped for a couple of Austrian hitchhikers, and made some questionable choices in terms of shortcuts, but remained unscathed.

I was trying to make time, so I had the little piece of crap really flying around the mountains and cliffs bordering the Brazilian coastline. We were on an uphill stretch, behind a painfully slow cement truck, for about three minutes, when I lost my patience and decided to floor it. I pulled left, downshifted into third, and slammed on the gas. Just as I was about two-thirds of my way past the puppy, a pick-up truck packed with what must have been four or five families spilling out the back appeared from the bend. They were tumbling downhill right at us at a cool forty-five miles an hour. I was fucked. I was already committed to the pass, on a narrow road, with no shoulder. I froze. He had too much momentum to break. If I went left, I'd hit the car. If I went right, I'd push both the cement truck and myself off the cliff.

The pick-up truck flew by, and I cut off the cement truck at a sharp angle. He slammed into us and fucked us up bad, but the truck was okay, and we were all alive.

With no insurance and a weekend bag of weed and pharmaceuticals in my trunk, I was thrown in a cell with forty other boondock criminals and spent six days and five nights in the Brazilian prison system. I was surrounded by rapists, killers, and thieves. Scared out of my fucking mind. A few guys looked like they were performing some sort of voodoo curses on the others and had floral, candlelit shrines set up around them. I demanded a lawyer, I screamed for *my rights. Hell, I even cried for my mother, but nothing worked. One guy punched me in the gut for making too much noise. The prisoners laughed at me, and the cops gave me a bill for $20,000 total in damages and bail.*

The next day, I was pulled out of the cell and brought into a questioning room. They tried to make me sign something that said "drogas" on it, and I refused. I would not admit to driving on any sort of drugs. I didn't take their piss tests either. My grave was dug deep enough, and I didn't want anything else on me. After hours of refusing their bullshit, two guards took me away and tossed me in a solitary cell. I yelled for the American Embassy, but they laughed. I thought I was stuck there forever.

The ceilings must have been about seven feet high, and the room was no bigger than a small closet. I couldn't even lie down. I didn't mind, though. It was dark, and it was lonely, but it was better than standing in the other cell with the real criminals, not that this room smelled any better. There was a clear stench of urine and vomit, and I could barely hold back my own gag reflex.

The story went on to explain my character's trials within the Brazilian prison system. It had nothing to do with the female perspective, but the teacher could not hold me accountable. She knew I hadn't signed up for her curriculum. I didn't care anyway. I was writing for my own enjoyment. All I could think about was Layla. As I debated how long was the right amount of time to wait to call, my phone buzzed. A text message.

"What? No call?" read the text. Layla.

I've never dialed a number so quickly.

"That was quick!" Layla teased. I knew I should have waited. She laughed at me for running away from her parents.

"You didn't tell on me, did you?"

"No way! It's not like I want them to know some boy slept over."

"So I'm just some boy?"

"You know what I mean. I said it was Lindsay."

I knew Mr. Semmering had seen me, but I dropped the subject. I asked her about tennis and told her about my short story. She asked to read it, and I reluctantly sent it over to her.

"You're really talented, Cal! That's so good!" A stretch. But I loved her for saying it. We spoke about nothing and everything, and I never wanted to hang up. I told her about how I got kicked out of Mather, and she already knew.

"No offense, but your friends are assholes for holding that grudge. It was as much their fault as yours, Cal. You were just helping them."

"I know," I said, "but, it really was dumb of me. I just wish I could go back and—"

"Get over it, Cal! You can't. You've got to move on!"

She wanted me to take her to the MOMA the next morning, but I had class. We even put our TVs on the same channel so we could watch some documentary on humpback whales at the same time. We didn't hang up until we realized it was already two in the morning.

"Lunch tomorrow?" I proposed. "Boathouse?"

"Deal."

I went to class the next morning for the first time in three weeks. Pretty much the same crowd from the last time. I wore a salmon-colored shirt and they all looked at me like I was a burn victim, but I didn't care. My face heated up and blushed when I saw Brenda, and I took the seat farthest away from her. We hadn't spoken since that night at my house a few of weeks before. She probably thought I was a jerk, but I was honestly just embarrassed. It didn't matter, though; could not compare her to Layla. The teacher made us all stand up and read our stories out loud. I was kind of excited about this.

Brenda read her's first. She wrote some crazy story in the voice of a nude Korai statue at the Met and how she hated everyone staring at her privates. Kind of weird, but cool. Another guy wrote a story from the perspective of an actual asshole having to take a shit every day. Definitely creative. As my turn approached, I realized that everyone was actually talented and that maybe I wasn't as great as I had thought.

I lost the urge to read and was thinking of ways to get out of there when Regina called my name. Fuck. I stood up straight, introduced my piece, took note of every critical eye in the room, and read. At first the room was pretty silent, which made me nervous, but then I started to hear a few laughs. It wasn't supposed to be funny. I guess people saw comic value in picturing the author in a Latin American prison. Anyway, I got through it, and the class applauded. Regina gave me an approving smile and approached me after class.

"That was very sharp, Callum. Nice job. You know, I've been thinking. You have not been around much, but I like your work. Between this and the piece you submitted on the first day, perhaps you should submit something to *Seasonal Beats* (the school's quarterly literary journal) for publication."

"Seriously?"

She nodded.

"Well, thanks!—I mean, yeah, I'll definitely work on some-thing."

I wanted to read more to my teacher but was empty handed. I picked up my notebook and thought about calling Layla.

Brenda was waiting for me at the door with a mischievous little smile, and I felt like an embarrassed ten-year-old boy.

"Hey, Brenda. How's it going?" I wasn't even going to make an excuse for not calling her.

"I loved your story, babe!"

"Thanks, it wasn't that good though. *Yours* was really awe-some. How did you think of that?"

We carried this polite banter down the elevator and out of the building. She played with the collar of my polo shirt.

"You look like my dad."

I doubted that, but whatever. I really just wanted to get home and go meet Layla.

"Allright, well, I'm out of here. Got to get home," I said.

"I'm actually heading uptown too . . . Want to take the subway together?"

"Sure, sounds good." Wouldn't hurt, and the subway would probably be quicker than a cab at midday anyway.

As we waited on the platform I noticed a tiny black girl in the corner singing "Ave Maria." She could really sing. Seriously, she had the loudest voice I'd ever heard. I was glad she was there, be-cause it took Brenda's attention too, and I could avoid forced con-versation. When the subway finally pulled in, I dropped five bucks into the girl's hat and darted in for an open seat. The train was filled to capacity, and our car was a veritable oven, producing some of the worst scents you could imagine. Body odor, bad cologne, a tuna sandwich, a little bit of wet wool, homeless filth, and urine.

An elderly Hispanic woman stood in front of me. She could barely keep her eyelids open. I knew that I should get up and give her my seat, but I was embarrassed to do it, so I waited for the next stop when people would be moving around, and it wouldn't look like a big deal.

Now standing, I turned around to where Brenda was leaning against the door and managed to place myself in a position where I was hovering in front of her. I tried balancing myself but kept stumbling. As gross as it was, I resorted to grabbing the pole to the right of me. Warm and greasy. I imagined how many people had already touched that piece of metal that day. How many people used their hands to blow their noses, wipe their asses, cough up their viruses, masturbate, touch raw foods, touch their pets, and then eventually rub their sweaty, slimy hands on this very pole. It was filthy. We stopped at Grand Central, and ten more people managed to squeeze themselves into the hot compartment of flesh, all different colors and consistencies. An overweight businessman behind me pushed me closer against the pole to the point where my body was pressed up against Brenda's. The pressure of her thigh gently aroused my penis to the point where she could definitely tell. She smiled. Fuck. This was awkward. I remember my body wanting her. I started looking at the ugly people on the train, tried reading the graffiti on the wall. I even thought about precalculus for a bit, but my eyes kept going back to Brenda and the cleavage coming out of her purple V-neck shirt. She purposely pressed her leg into me at every bump or turn of the subway, and I was starting to breathe kind of heavily. A cold gust from the air conditioning blew through and gave my nose a little itch. It quickly became a nuisance, as I didn't want to touch my face. I tried rubbing my shoulder against my nostril, but that just irritated it more. The itch was building up horribly, and I knew I was going to have to sneeze. I would just redirect it through my mouth and swallow, I thought. No big deal. The train turned, and Brenda sent a shiver up my body to the point where I had to smile. Whoops . . . a—A—A-CHOOO! And I watched a beige, gooey booger shoot out of my left nostril with a wet "swiffp" and dart directly toward Brenda's forearm in slow motion. Slap.

I didn't raise my head. I just stood there watching the glimmering piece of snot dance and wobble on her tan skin. Gross. I looked up and apologized but she was laughing it off and wiping her arm on the pole. What a piece of work.

Brenda kept playing her little leg game as we approached 86th Street, but I wanted nothing to do with it.

"So I don't have to be anywhere for another hour or so. I've got some nug, if you want to go back to your place and smoke or . . . hang out," Brenda offered.

That was it. She was offering sex. It was so easy. I could have lost my virginity right there and then. A week ago I would have ravaged her, but I had to meet Layla. I did not know it at the time, but this was one of my bigger and wiser decisions. I thought of last time we hooked up, and for some reason I thought of Miralva, and I thought of the snot, and most importantly, I thought of Layla. This girl had nothing on her.

"No thanks, I'm pretty beat. I actually think I'm going to take a nap."

She got the picture; I could tell she was a little embarrassed. It would be the last time Brenda and I ever spoke.

I jumped off the train on 86th Street and jogged home. I leaped up the steps, two at a time, threw off my clothes, and took a quick shower before heading to the Boathouse.

28

THE BOATHOUSE

I JUMPED OUT OF THE cab and entered Central Park, veering right onto the loop. I walked slowly because I didn't want to work up a sweat again before seeing Layla, but deliberately because I wanted to be on time. It was Thursday, so I was hopeful there wouldn't be too many tourists.

I walked through the cast-iron gate, down the shady path, and into the restaurant.

"Hi there. Table for two, please, maybe something by the water?"

The maître d' asked me to hold on a moment and I started to re-tuck my shirt into my pants. Suddenly, I felt a hand deep in my pocket.

"Don't say a word. Money. Now. All of it."

I froze and looked forward before slowly turning to see Layla keeling over in laughter.

"Wow. You should have seen yourself! How brave!"

I stood there stupefied.

"Okay, okay. You got me. *Not* funny, but you got me."

"Actually, *very* funny! I'm sorry."

My heart started to settle down. The host led us to a sunny table overlooking the lake. I looked across the room, thankful to see the restaurant was half empty.

"I'm so glad you picked this place. My dad used to take me here all the time."

I wasn't sure that was exactly what I was going for. "Hmm. Well I *do* try to keep things sexy."

"Shush. I didn't mean it like that. I really like it. Did you know that this was built as an actual boathouse in the 1870s?" she asked.

"I didn't, but that *does* make sense given the name."

"Stop." She smiled. "My dad is a huge history buff. You can't walk around New York with him without getting an earful. He used to pick me up after school, when he could, and make me walk everywhere but home talking about everything from fur trading to architecture to sea battles on the Hudson. Mom still calls him the professor."

"And that was fun?" I couldn't picture anything like that with my parents.

"Well, he would bribe me with ice cream!"

I hesitantly asked for the wine menu and prayed that the waiter would not card me. He didn't, and I exhaled. The names were all foreign, and I realized I had no idea if Layla even wanted a drink.

"How about a bottle of Veuve?" I suggested more timidly than I wanted.

Layla put her water down and laughed. "Who are you?"

"What?"

"Champagne? Are we celebrating?"

"Well, sure. I mean. No. I mean. I—"

"Are we on Nicky Beach? Bottle service? Where is the DJ?" Layla teased.

I felt like an idiot. She ordered a ginger ale, and I did the same.

"Any word how Collin is doing?" Layla asked. "That was too much."

"Oh yeah. I forgot to tell you. He claims he does not remember a thing, but woke up with remnants of vomit on his dinner jacket. He could barely speak the next day. Poor guy."

"Oh no. Collin. Always two steps ahead of himself. He didn't ask about me—I mean us, or anything, did he? I don't care. It's just that. I love him, but he's a bit of a gossip, you know, and—"

"Don't worry, don't worry. I didn't say anything," I replied, forgetting Collin had put his own version of two and two together.

"Okay, great! Did you have fun the other night?"

"Yes! I mean. I had fun with you. A blast really. It was a little tough leading up to then, though. I don't really want to go into it again, but my friends are such dicks."

"I know, Cal. We don't have to talk about it. I told you. It's not your fault. Water under the bridge, and if they are real friends, they'll get over it."

"Thanks, Layla." Though I desperately wanted more reassurance, it meant a lot that she was being a friend.

Layla finished her Caesar salad, I devoured my soft-shell crabs, and we actually decided to have a glass of wine. As we both stared over the weeping willows to the high rises on Central Park South, I sensed that Layla wanted something.

"So are you going to take me for a ride?"

"What do you mean?" I pretended I didn't know what she was talking about.

"In a rowboat, of course! Isn't that half of this date? she smiled.

"Oh, I'm sorry. You think this is a date?" I responded in a deadpan voice.

She cocked her head and smiled.

"Please?"

I *really* did not want to do this. A rowboat in the middle of the City? I looked around. The restaurant was empty.

"Fine. Why not?"

I paid the bill, and I prayed nobody would see us as we walked outside toward the boats.

"Ahoy, sailor." I laughed, hopping in first to sit in the stern.

"Ahoy, captain," Layla took my hand to ease herself in. Her tan legs glistened under her white lace skirt and she caught me staring. We both smirked.

"Staring at something?" Layla looked down at her horizontal-striped blue and white long-sleeve tee. "I actually do kind of look nautical, don't I?"

"You look great," I responded too eagerly. She blushed.

"So how was class, anyway?

"Actually, it was kind of awesome." I was cautious of breaking a sweat and rowed us close to shore under a tree. "I read one of my stories, and the teacher suggested that I submit it to the program's literary magazine."

"Callum, that is amaz—"

We were cut off by a booming voice shouting my last name from roughly twenty yards away.

I turned around and saw Thomas, Owen, Branson, and Chuck all sitting around a table at the outside bar cracking into their first beers.

"Shit. I'm sorry Layla. Mather guys, who . . ."

"Don't worry about it. Ignore them."

I was a sitting duck.

"This is ADORABLE, Littlefield!" shouted Branson.

"Your girlfriend on your list too, asshole?" Fucking Thomas.

I apologized again to Layla. Layla leaned over and squeezed my knee, but I couldn't look at her.

"Let's go home," she said. "I have to run some errands anyway."

I rowed us back to shore, stifling the fury and humiliation rising up in my chest.

"Aweee. Date's over? Gonna go get 'er done, big guy?" Chuck cackled.

I shook my head and apologized again as I awkwardly struggled ringing the oars out of the water. We walked out of the park.

"Callum, you really don't have to worry about this."

"I'm fine." They were being idiots and did not mean real harm. I could have been in their shoes too, but at the time, my hate had no limit. I put Layla in a taxi and closed the door harder than I had meant to.

"Call me tomorrow?" Layla peered through the window.

"Yes. Again. I'm sorry."

I called Layla later on that night, still embarrassed for what had happened. I started to dial, but noticed my heavy breathing. This happened a few times—pick-up, dial, breathe, change my mind—until finally let it ring. Her voicemail picked up: shit. I hung up, defeated.

29

RUMOR MILL

ANNOYED BY HER RUNAWAY grandchild, Grandmaman began to call the New York house more often. Two days later, I was back on Long Island, nervously avoiding Miralva. Still not a word from Layla. I began to panic. I slacked on my work around the property, I went out for food, I watched movies, I slept, and I checked my phone every ten minutes. I couldn't call Layla's cell phone anymore. I already looked pressed, and I didn't want to cross the stalker line. Trouble was that I couldn't think of anything else. I was obsessed. And I felt like a chick. This is what chicks did. What was wrong with me? I finally decided that her cell phone was broken and I needed to call her house.

I tried information, but she wasn't listed, so I went to the kitchen and pulled out the Social Register. A little outdated and pathetic, I know, but this time, the black, leather-bound status symbol actually came in handy. I picked up the phone.

A man answered.

"Hi. This is Callum. May I please speak to Layla?" A heavy pause with no response.

"Sure, just a second, Callum," he finally replied.

The Semmerings kept me on hold for a solid four minutes. I thought they might have forgotten I was on the line. I wanted to hang up and call back, but I was too embarrassed. I would hang up if it hit six minutes. What could they have been talking about? I could just picture it . . .

"Oh, Callum. You know? The boy who was masturbating to the picture of your mother in the bathroom when we returned home the other day and was too chicken to introduce himself. That is the boy who is on the phone."

Man, I was scum. How could I even talk to Layla then? What if she knew? Is that why she hadn't called back? No, she couldn't have. Nobody saw me. The housekeeper? No chance. Door was shut. What about the window, though? Maybe their neighbo—

"Hello?" She finally picked up.

"Oh, hey! It's Callum," I said in an overly enthusiastic voice.

"Hi, Callum. I'm sorry I didn't call you back. I've been kind of busy."

"Oh, no worries." Something was off in her voice. I was forcing the conversation, telling stupid stories about Mather and my pseudo-important friends. She was not entertained. I asked her obvious questions, and she gave me curt answers.

"So I was thinking we could get together for tennis tomorrow afternoon. I want to see that serve you were bragging about."

"Oh, yeah. I actually sprained my ankle yesterday. It's pretty bad."

"Oh, that sucks, I'm sorry. Lunch instead?

"I'm babysitting. It's actually a pretty tough week."

"Oh, no worries. Well maybe we could go to the Philharmonic in the park together next Tuesday?" She had to bite on this one.

"I don't think so, Callum. I'm not really into that stuff."

What the fuck was going on?

"Um, look, I know we just met, but what's wrong? I thought we had a great time the other night. I'm still sorry about my friends in the park, they're idiots, but I know you love the Philharmonic in the park. You mentioned it yourself." Pause.

"I changed my mind."

"Did *I* do something wrong?" I asked.

"Apparently we didn't have enough of a good time the other night because you had to go around telling all of your stupid friends that you slept with me. I gotta go."

The line went dead. My heart sank into the pit of my stomach.

Patterson.

Fucking fucking Patterson.

I slammed the phone down and stopped myself from throwing it across the room.

"Yooo hooo. Mosquitio," my Grandmother called, as she rang her bell.

Why now?

"I'd like to take a bath."

Not what I wanted to think about at the moment. I was mortified, ready to absolutely murder Patterson.

"Be down in a bit, Grandmaman."

I called Layla back and left her a message pleading my innocence and trying to explain that people just liked to spread gossip. I knew she wouldn't return my call. My elaborate message sounded like a lie anyway. I dialed Patterson.

"Sorry man, I thought you told me you fucked her. And I only told Courtney." Courtney Peters was a girl Patterson had been hooking up with off and on throughout high school.

"Dude, I said I slept AT her apartment. On a couch in *full* formal attire! I didn't even remove my cuff links. And fuck that, you knew Courtney would tell everyone. She's the fucking information line of the Upper East Side! Fuck!"

"Relax, bro. Seriously. My bad."

"Yoooo hooo!" my grandmother yelled again.

"Forget it, I have to run."

"By the way, dude, not to piss you off anymore, but I heard again that kid Brooks has been saying he took her down."

"Thanks, Patterson."

I hung up and walked down the hall. What a dick. I bathed my grandmother and then assisted her into a faded yellow gown, not saying anything about its deteriorating lining.

"You look really pretty, Grandmaman."

Leaving her at her makeup table, I went to the other room to make some feeler calls. Apparently everyone had heard the same thing. I did what I could to clear things up, just hoping my efforts would get back to Layla. Still, days passed and no calls. After a bit of digging, I later found out from a girl I used to see that she had also heard that Layla was hooking up with that Princeton guy, Brooks. Patterson was right. It was over.

I had no choice but to put everything into work. When we were young, the Octopus used to keep the cousins busy by having us make paths through the woods. We would plan them, weed them, and then line them with shells and stones from the beach. It didn't matter where they went as long as they were neat and precise. We eventually built a maze and called it the "Secret Forest." I completed more paths that week than I had in countless summers on the Island. Some went to the tennis court, some went in circles, and some even went onto other people's property. I didn't care where they went. They just kept my body away from Miralva and my thoughts away from Layla. When I had made enough paths to confuse any visitor, I decided to rebuild the small bridge that covered the rain stream near the driveway. The Octopus and I had built this bridge together when I was five and named it "Callum's Bridge," but it had since rotted and fallen apart. I collected wood from around the property and replaced each rotten step with a firm new piece of timber. It was small. Five feet by three feet to be exact, but I was proud of the finished product. I even sanded its handrails. Grandmaman didn't notice any of my work, as hurricane season was upon us and she was fixed to the weather channel like glue. Still, I knew she would have been pleased.

As time passed, the Octopus started coming to me more frequently with bizarre requests. One time she wanted me to buy lumber to rebuild the chicken coop. The next day she wanted me to pick up a package of clothing for Aurelio somewhere in the middle of Queens. A few days later I had to go buy her new undergarments. It didn't matter. It's not like I had anything else going on.

Things became uncomfortable again. I found Miralva pacing the hallways one night and could swear I heard her humming outside my room on two separate occasions. Grandmaman was also slipping more. I went to the City one evening and when I came back, I noticed at lunch that she was wearing the same gown and jewels that she had worn the night before. The Octopus never dressed up for lunch and would never repeat the same outfit like that. I asked her why she hadn't changed.

"Oh you *don't* think I'm beautiful anymore Mosquito. Is that it?"

I put my head down and hugged her. "Of course you are, Octopus," I whispered softly. Just then, I looked up and saw Miralva smiling at us from the other room. She quickly turned her head and walked away.

I was weeding a path later that afternoon when I saw Miralva picking wildflowers down the hill. She was singing the same song I had heard in the hallways. This was not right.

I pulled Berta aside the next morning and told her I was leaving. She looked disappointed. "Well, it's hard to explain, but I have to get out of here. That being said, I'm worried about Grandmaman, Berta. Please keep a close eye on her okay?"

"Everything's fine. This is normal," she assured me. She was wrong though. The Octopus was drifting.

I wasn't back in town for more than a week when I heard that Grandmaman had ratted out my abrupt departure to my parents. They were due to return in less than a month and were not pleased. First my dad left a message in that same dry and disappointed voice.

"Callum, I don't know what you're thinking, but you are seriously pushing it. What are you *doing*? You're screwing up your name, which is just about all . . . Listen. You just really have to get back on track and stop this bullshit. I'll try you again soon."

He thought I was driving them away. He thought I was an emotional recluse that didn't care about my future or the world. He was wrong. I cared. I wish they knew the shit I had to deal with at that house. I brushed off his message. He was right in that I didn't share the same cares and concerns as them anymore. Either way, he'd never understand me unless I shut up and followed his lead. There was no point in explaining. I just accepted his disenchanted voice and moved forward.

My mother's message was just as thwarted.

"Callum, it's your mother." Her voice was competing with background conversation.

"Do you have *any* idea how much we've spent on you?" I heard glasses clink in the background and realized she was at a bar. "Hundreds of thousands of dollars, and you throw it all away. I don't know *what* to *do* with you anymore!" Her words began to slur as she lost composure. So much for good cop. "Do you *hate* us? Is that it? You hate me? *Why* do you insist on ruining everything?"

I bit my lip and looked at the answering machine in silence. She didn't mean all of that. I reached out, erased the message, and put my face in my hands as I braced for the next one. I really was a waste. I vowed to never feel like a leach again.

Her next message came a few hours later.

"Callum, I am sorry for the way I spoke to you earlier." Her voice was thin and weak. Maybe she'd slept off her afternoon tantrum. "I love you so much, and I'm really worried about you. You don't understand that you're still a boy and need someone to take care of you. Please return to Long Island before anything else happens." They'd do anything to get me back to the Octopus. They really thought I was going to get into more trouble and heaven forbid have my name float around the Upper East Side gossip circuit again. *Why* did they care so much? I wasn't going to do anything wrong.

Her last message was frantic and desperate, without anything to say.

"Callum." Gulp. "Your father and I are very worried about your situation. Go back to your grandmother's house immediately. You're making everyone sick with worry, and I don't want to have to tell the whole family about this mess. We don't even know what you're doing there! Nobody has heard from you, and it's not fair."

I spent my mournful, lonely days writing apology drafts to Layla, never to be sent out. Getting my admiration and disgust on paper almost gave me a sense of accomplishment. Industrious almost. I was seeing reason in my emotions. I decided that I had to do something, I just didn't know what.

That night, I sat in the study watching a movie about firefighters and ordered Chinese food. Chicken with broccoli, fried pork dumplings, and mushu pancakes. I've ordered the same thing since I was nine. I decided to call the Octopus to let her know I was all right.

"Hi, Grandmaman. It's me, Callum."

Pause.

"Well, I don't have much to say to you, Callum."

"I know, it's just that my parents—"

"Stop it, Callum. Are you coming home? I don't have very much to say to you right now."

"I'm sorry Grandmaman. I know you are upset that I left, but I have been busy with my schoolwork and can't concentrate very well out there."

"Come off it, Mosquito. You know I'm harder to fool." She was right. I could bullshit pretty much anybody in my family except for her. She always saw right through me.

"Fine. It's a girl. She's really great, but I think I've ruined it."

"Well, Mosquito . . . that I believe. We women have the power to make any man a fool. I used to drive your grandfather absolutely mad. Oh, how I was mean! Hehe," she laughed. "Now to fix it, you have to embrace the facts and take into account that great love involves great risk. If she is special then it should be a fight to get her." The spirit in her voice had returned.

I let that marinate for a while. She was right, I never took risks, and I was being a pussy. I was feeling sorry for myself and doing nothing when I should have been acting. I thanked the Octopus and told her I had to deal with some stuff but would be back out there as soon as I could.

The next morning I called Flessas Flower Shop on 92nd and Madison and ordered three dozen white and yellow roses. I didn't know anything about flowers, but the lady at the other end giggled and told me that the order would be more than enough to say I like you, and I'm sorry. She could tell my predicament was pretty severe. I told the lady to include a note:

Dear Layla,

I'm an inconsiderate, pathetic, moronic, immature jerk to even insinuate anything that could create such a horrible misunderstanding. You can't imagine my overwhelming self repulse. Please accept my apology and this token of my affection. Thinking of you.

Yours,
Callum

I called her that night.

"You're such a dork," she said, without a hello. "But you're cute."

It worked.

I told her everything, and she agreed to have a drink with me at Dorrian's later that week. I was back in business.

30

DORRIAN'S

WHY THE *FUCK* DID I say we'd go to Dorrian's? I couldn't get into Dorrian's if my life depended on it. No way would Patterson's ID work there. I met Layla in front of her building. She wore Belgian loafers with no socks, a white sleeveless shirt, and green pants. We made a left on 84th Street toward Second Avenue.

"You know, we don't have to go to D's if you don't want to, Layla. It might be kind of dead. Would you rather go to a restaurant or something and grab a bottle of wine?"

"No, no, Cal! I've never been. I think it will be fun. I've heard it's a blast. Besides, I made a ten-dollar bet with my dad that I could get in. He still thinks I'm twelve."

"He doesn't care?"

"That I'm going to a bar four blocks from home that's probably filled with his friends' kids? Hah, no. He has bigger fish to fry. Mom's money is on me too."

"That's awesome." I imagined my parent's reaction. They knew I drank and went out and everything, but we kind of had an unwritten rule not to acknowledge anything.

I had heard about the Dorrian's lore as well. The bar was an institution and local watering hole for three generations of Upper East Side animals. I was ahead of my skis though and knew the bar was at least two or three years away. I had no chance of getting in.

"Okay, okay. We're going."

Layla and I reached 84th and Second and saw a huge crowd of colorful shirts and jeans across the street. The bar's windows were open and eighties music blasted out onto the street. My heart started racing.

"Packed for karaoke night, I guess." I motioned to a poster of non-descript blondes singing into a microphone. "We better get on line."

We lined up against the windowed wall about fifteen people back from the door. I was easily the youngest-looking guy on the corner. How was I going to pull this off? Do I tip the bouncer? How much? What was his name? My sister had told me there were two bouncers, Kenny and Rey, but I wasn't sure who was who.

James the bum ran across the street, through traffic, waving one arm at me and holding his boom box in the other.

"C—motha fucka! What you doin' here? I'm tell yo mortha if you don't cough it up, motha fucka." No no no. Negative attention. I gave James ten bucks to walk away.

"Hah! You *know* him?!" Layla laughed." I see that guy everywhere!" I guess James' turf expanded to the Second Avenue bars after dark. Made sense. There he could still collect tolls from the clients that had grown out of Carnegie Hill. Seems that people were more generous after a few drinks too.

"Yah, my network spreads pretty wide . . . hah. He's been hanging around our block forever."

Three guys in their midtwenties and loafers were smoking cigarettes a few feet away from us and checking out Layla. I pretended to ignore them. "Oh my God, check out that girl." I pointed inside at a blonde in white jeans and a blue shirt rocking out with the microphone in one hand and a tambourine in the other. She was belting out Tina Turner's "Proud Mary" and killing it.

We inched forward, and I saw a short brunette in a white tube top and jeans run out of the bar holding her phone to her ear.

"Hold on one sec," she squealed and then walked over to the window right in front of me, banged on the frame, and screamed, "Lindsay! How many do you want? Really? Just one? We have that Africa benefit tomorrow and then it will be a pain to get anything in Long Island this weekend. OKAY. Got it!" She stepped back from the window and spoke back into the phone. "Hey, sorry about that. Six white T-shirts. How long? Okay, forty minutes? Ugh. Okay. No, no, not in front. In between First and Second. I'm in a white tube top." She hung up the phone and walked back into the bar without hesitation.

Layla rolled her eyes.

"Seriously?"

I had not even been paying any attention to the transaction. I was too busy thinking about how we were going to get in.

Twenty minutes later, we were next in line. I stood as tall as I could, looking up at Kenny or Rey guarding the door. He must have been six foot seven, three hundred and fifty pounds. His leather jacket could have served as a tent for two normal people, and his silver watch was a belt for heavyset children.

"No more guys!" he yelled to the crowd. "Only ladies. We're filled up." Shit. I stepped aside as four horsey girls in pastels rushed to the front of the line and jumped in.

"Sir. I'm sorry, but is there any chance my friend and I can get in? We've been waiting forever," I asked. He looked at Layla and smiled.

"She can."

"Great!" and I started walking past him until he put his catcher's mitt hand on my chest.

"Nope. No more dudes."

Four tall guys in blazers and jeans brushed in front of me and walked in. One of them was Al Timson, who was a senior at Mather when I was a freshman. We didn't acknowledge each other.

"What's up, Rey."

"Good to see you, Rey."

"Thanks man."

"Rey REY!"

I looked back up at him. "What about those guys, man?"

"Regulars. I told you. She's good, but I can't help you." I looked over at Layla and she shrugged her shoulders.

"You should go, Layla. I don't want to you to lose your bet, and I'll catch up with you later."

She smiled.

"Give me a break! The bet with my *parents*? Let's get out of here." And she grabbed my arm and hailed a cab in a surprisingly smooth motion. "73rd and First, please."

"Session's?" It was the notoriously underage bar on 73rd Street.

"Yeah I think it'll be fun! There'll be people there."

We arrived at Session's and Layla marched right in, no problem. I followed her closely but ran into another muscle-bound doorkeeper.

"ID?"

"Yeah, sure." The bouncer took a long look down at Patterson's ID, back at me, and then at the card again.

"You sure this is you?"

"Yes. Definitely."

"You got any backup?"

Fuck. I went back to my wallet and pulled out my credit card with my real name on it.

"You know, sir, I actually don't. This is my stepfather's credit card, and I don't have anything else with my name on it."

"Get out of here, man. Nice try." And he shoved both cards into my chest.

I didn't know what to do. I didn't want Layla to know I got rejected, but I didn't want to ditch her either. Maybe I'd go home and send her a text message that I was feeling sick. I stuck out my arm for a cab when I felt my phone vibrate against my leg. It was a text from Layla.

Come around the corner to 73rd Street in the back.

Of course, the back door. Rejected, yes, but not defeated. I walked around the corner and down the dark street to the garbage dump beside the bar. I could hear the suppressed music from the inside and hoped I would not have to wait long.

A huge steel side door suddenly swung open, and the sounds of a Guns N' Roses cover band blasted out onto the street.

"Get in here!" Layla yelled over the music. I ran inside and Layla gave me a hug.

"Thanks! Sorry this has been such a hassle."

"Don't worry. We're here!" Layla took my wrist and dragged me to the bar. "Guess who's at the bar?!" Patterson was saddled up with the Bellatini twins and a round of tequila shots. No wonder the bouncer didn't believe it was me.

"Make it two more," I yelled to the bartender as I slapped Patterson on the back and kissed both of the twins on the cheek.

"What's up man?! How's it going?"

"Not bad, brotha. Crushing it!" Patterson gave me a high five and pulled me into whispering distance. "Glad to see you pulled it together with Semmering, stud."

"No problem, buddy. All good."

The bartender gave us our shots, salt, and lime, and Patterson lifted up his glass.

"Here is to drinking triple, seeing double, and acting single!"

"You're an ass." Layla said. "You know Courtney actually likes you? Don't ask me why."

"Woah, woah, woah, easy Layla. I like her too. We have a good thing going. Relax!"

Layla gave him a disgusted look as he downed his shot and loudly smacked his lips.

"Big night, guys. Big night!"

The Bellatinis and I followed suit with our shots, but Layla passed me hers and whispered "thank you" so nobody else could see.

I smiled and took hers as well.

"You okay there?" Layla asked one of the twins, as she clumsily grabbed a stranger's beer for a chaser.

"I'm fine." And she slid off her stool and headed toward the bathroom.

"Guess some people just can't hold their liquor like the rest of us, huh, champ?" Patterson put his arm on my shoulder.

"Hah, yeah *right* buddy. Coming from the guy hurling off of the Zoo cruise!"

"I was seasick, man. Give me a break. Food poisoning. Fucking crab cakes."

"Yeah that was real cute, Collin . . ." Layla laughed and grabbed my arm. "Let's go dance."

Layla and I picked up right where we left off from the party.

I had her spinning all over the dance floor, and my air guitar let out a face-melting solo. We got closer at every song, and I snuck in a kiss after dipping her during "Sweet Child O' Mine."

"I've got to run to the bathroom. Will be right back," she said after pulling away. Maybe it was too soon to kiss her? I took the opportunity to go as well and found a men's room no bigger than a standard closet packed with five bodies. One of them was in a stall behind a sliding door that would not close all the way. Two others stood in front trying to block the open view for their friend.

"Give me your key, dude," came the voice from behind the stall.

"Sure. Just hurry the fuck up," said door-blocker number one.

An elderly Bill Cosby lookalike sat on a stool by the sink and offered me a mint.

"No thanks. Just waiting for the toilet."

I heard a few sniffs and a "Whooooo. There she is!" and out came Patterson from behind the door.

"Dude. You're ridiculous!" I said. "Could you be any louder?"

"Don't worry about it, bro. Herbert here has me covered." Patterson passed a white bag to one of his stall guardians and tossed the bathroom attendant a twenty.

"No problem. Just here to pass out towels and candies." Herbert smiled and motioned to his basket of mints.

"Want a bump, bro? I got an eight ball and am set for the night," Patterson offered.

"Naw. I'm cool, man, thanks."

"Then let's get the fuck out of this bathroom! Can't freaking breath in here."

"I'll see you out there, buddy." I gave Patterson a high five and watched him walk out, slapping the walls on either side of him.

I used the toilet, washed my hands, left the bathroom, and

saw Layla standing in the hall looking angry as ever. Oh shit. I *really* shouldn't have kissed her.

"Something wrong?"

"No. Ugh! I just stepped in a *HUGE* puddle of barf. Can we please get out of here? I'm sorry. This is just too gross. One of the twins threw up all over the place." Relieved, I led us out the front door.

Layla and I went to a pizza parlor down the block to grab a slice for the two of us and napkins for her shoes. I did the best I could to clean them up, but they still smelled rancid.

"Let's get you home. These are just nasty."

"Good idea, Cal. You're sweet. Thanks."

Layla leaned her head on my shoulder in the cab ride home, and I thought about how I would kiss her. I breathed into my hand and smelt pepperoni. Shit. I should have taken one of those mints from the bathroom attendant. My hands were cold, and my arm fell asleep under the weight of Layla's head. I flexed a bit to try and get the blood running but didn't want her to notice.

"Thanks for taking my shot and really so much for everything tonight, Cal. Sorry we had to take off early," Layla apologized as we pulled up to her building.

"Give me a break. Thanks for getting me in! I had a blast." That was my chance. I had to do it then. I leaned in. Paused. Leaned back out. "It really was fun." Come on Callum, do it. I leaned in, and Layla turned her face, kissed me on the cheek, and gave me a long embrace.

A hug? Did I blow it? Was I in the friend zone? Layla opened her door to get out, and I grabbed her wrist.

"Hey, Layla, how about dinner tomorrow night?" She smiled and kissed me again on the cheek.

"Sure."

31

TRANNIES

I PLANNED OUT EVERY detail for our date. I was not going to fuck this one up. It had to be perfect. She was taking the train in from Greenwich, where she had been visiting a friend for the day, so I told her I'd pick her up from Grand Central then head downtown. I thought about telling her to get off at 125th Street, since that is so much closer to home, but it felt wrong to tell her to get off in Harlem.

I pulled up to the west entrance of the magnificent Vander-bilt structure and double-parked across the street. It was seven o'clock and her train was supposed to get in at 7:09. I fumbled through the radio stations for something she might like. Classic rock was cool, but too standard. I flipped to the end of a great Temptations song, but thought our parents' music was too dorky. Rap, no. Latin? Maybe interesting. I finally resorted to Z100, the cheesy Top 40 radio station that everybody listened to, and turned down the volume.

7:09 came and went and she still wasn't around. Relax, I thought. The train was probably just pulling up. I could not remember if I had put on deodorant or not. I put my right hand through my shirt and under my armpit to check things out. I was perspiring a little bit, but I sniffed my hand and didn't smell bad. Okay. Phew. Probably just nerves. I checked myself out in the rearview mirror a few times. My hair was pissing me off. I tried matting it down with a little spit and was just getting it to work when—KNOCK KNOCK.

Whoa. Crap. My elbow slammed the window and my heart skipped a beat as I wiped saliva down my cheek. I snapped my neck to the left, and there she was, laughing at me. My finger began opening the window for a second until I realized how stupid that was and finally opened the door.

"Hey, Layla!" She looked hotter than any girl I had ever seen. I tried to get out as suavely as possible. She was wearing a teal blue silk dress with a Nehru collar. It pushed up her perfect breasts and hugged her tight stomach and round little ass. I couldn't stop staring. Her cheeks were sun kissed and smooth. Her eyes matched the blue silk of her dress. I just wanted to grab her right then and there, lift her onto on the hood of the car and start kissing, but she wasn't a touchy type. I gave her a hug and a deliberate kiss on the cheek and then opened the passenger door for her. We were off.

I crossed over to Fifth and started a few blocks down toward the restaurant. I had a 7:45 reservation for us at a popular new spot in the East Village called Lucky Chang's. The menu was a tropical Asian fusion cuisine, but the place was known for its entertainment. Layla didn't know it yet, as it had only opened last month, but I was taking her to a transvestite-themed restaurant. Apparently, all of the waiters were men dressed as women and the whole evening was a big stage show.

"How are the shoes?"

"Ugh—still so gross. I think I'm going to have to throw them out. And I loved them *so* much. Whatever. Thanks though."

"Don't mention it. Last night was fun." Short pause. "So I think you're really going to like this place, Layla. It's supposed to be pretty awesome."

"I'm sure I will, Cal—as long as my dinner partner can go easy on his *boooaarding* school stories . . ."

"Touché—like *you're* so bohemian." I rolled my eyes. "Well we're downtown, aren't we? That's a step, isn't it, Soon Foo?" and I motioned to her dress.

She smiled and slapped my hand away. A genuine tight-cheeked ear-to-ear smile.

Then something horrible happened. I really should have planned for it, but the thought hadn't even crossed my mind. After a few blocks of New York City stop-and-go traffic, I realized that I was getting a huge erection. Well . . . an erection. I don't know why, but this always happens to me out of nowhere. Especially in cars. I wasn't fully standing just yet, but it was to the point that I could make it sit up at my will and back down again when I held my breath and loosened my stomach muscles. It was uncomfortable, to say the least. To make matters worse, I was wearing Diesel jeans that gave me no excess space. Layla was looking right at my face as we made conversation about architecture (my mind was far from the topic), and if she looked down for just one second she would have noticed my throbbing member trying to push through thick uncomfortable denim around my legs. It was painful and slightly humiliating. I had to think fast.

"If you look down on the right of this next cross street, you can just barely see one of my favorite buildings. It's an old bank converted into a hotel. Really pretty sick." I motioned to a street filled with parking lots, fast food restaurants, and a fictional hotel, while I quickly tucked myself up under my belt, all in one motion.

"I don't see it! Where?"

"Aw, must have missed it. Sorry. It's really hard to see from this angle."

We finally reached the restaurant just before 7:30, but there wasn't a parking spot in site. I should have thought of that. For some reason, I had a very optimistic attitude that the village would be full of parking spots. Maybe I didn't believe people with cars really lived down there.

"Do you want me to get out and grab our table?" Layla offered. "So we don't miss our reservation?"

Fuck. Come on. There had to be one near by.

"No, no, no. That's not necessary. Well figure something out."

Five more minutes of this and I felt that the evening was in jeopardy, so I found a parking lot four blocks away and threw some stranger the keys for twenty-five bucks an hour. By the time we got to the restaurant it was almost eight o'clock.

The restaurant was a sensory overload. Seventies music blasted into our ears, and we were suddenly in a bizarre world somewhere in between Hong Kong, Jamaica, and South Beach. You should have seen Layla's head cock to the left with curiosity when she saw the maître d', but she quickly overcame her surprise with a closed-mouth smile and a glance in my direction.

"Hello, cutie. May I help you?" The six foot four, two hundred and fifty pound black man in a Madonna costume asked me as he adjusted his silver cone-shaped breasts.

"Yes, reservation for two under Littlefield, please."

The drag queen looked at his little black book for a lengthy minute. Silence. I looked forward: Please, please, please don't tell us that we missed our table. I really didn't want to ruin this. I think he could tell too, because the man honestly did look sad when he turned back up and told us that they had given our table away. This sucked. He told us to wait by the bar and that he would try to work something out, but he could not make any promises.

"I'm so sorry, Layla. I really should have planned this out better."

"Stop it! It's fine! This place is hysterical. Let's have a drink." Layla ordered a fruity martini and I had a Stoli soda. The bar was packed and I didn't want us to wait for long, so I took matters into my own hands.

I had seen my dad tip before. He always knew a guy. It used to embarrass me, but then I realized that it was actually pretty convenient. I had seen him take the folded bill from his jacket pocket and seamlessly slip it from his hand to someone else's hundreds of times. A magician. I could do it no problem. I excused myself away from Layla for a second, walked toward the corner so nobody would see me taking out my wallet, pulled out a twenty and two tens (I didn't think twenty would be sufficient in my case), folded them together, and made my return for big black Madonna.

"Excuse me, sir . . . I mean ma'am." He didn't hear.

"Excuse me," I repeated. Still no response. So, I leaned over and tapped him on the shoulder. THWACK! He smacked my arm away so that one of the tens fell on the floor by his feet.

"Can't you see I'm busy, kid?" He hissed as I picked up the

semi folded bill by his heels. He looked down, saw me fumbling for the cash, and apologized. I managed to pull the money and myself together and looked him in the eye.

"Don't worry about it. My fault for hassling you. I am just in the middle of a very special evening and would really appreciate it if you could find us a table." I shook the man's hand, giving him the forty dollars.

"Ohhhhh you are just too precious!" responded the man in a big Southern voice. "Let's see what we can do."

Luckily, Layla hadn't noticed any bit of that embarrassing exchange, and we were led to our table within minutes. As we walked to our seats, I saw various men breaking their necks on Layla. At first it pissed me off, but then again I kind of liked it. Everyone noticed the prettiest girl in the room, and she was with me.

"You really do look delightful."

I shouldn't have said that. She blushed, and it became a little bit awkward. Nothing a little wine couldn't fix, though. I scanned the menu for the third cheapest bottle and ordered us a pinot grigio. Layla made an overtly sophisticated face as I tasted from the glass, causing me to crack up and spit out a little.

"Will you please stop? I'm trying to get a sense of the tones," I retorted.

"Oh *reeaaallly,* Mr. Littlefield? Please. Indulge me."

"Well, it is a touch oakie with a hint of berries. *Very* unassuming."

"Hah, you're so full of it."

Layla smiled as the waiter topped off our glasses. I soon realized that I was about three drinks deep and that I should cut myself off, since I was driving.

"Besides, I'm carrying precious cargo."

"You're such a dork!" she winced.

I liked how she called out my bullshit. A waiter served me my chicken with broccoli, and I took one large gulp of wine and managed to ask her, "So Layla, I don't mean to be nosy, but who is this Brooks guy I've been hearing about?"

She stared at me blankly and then looked like she might cry.

"He's a guy I know. Really an ass. Our parents are friends, but that—"

And suddenly Layla had a huge dick and two balls all packaged up in silver nylon presented about four inches away from her mouth. One of the show girls had done a handstand and then wrapped his legs around my date while blowing a whistle, signaling that the show was about to begin. Smoke was coming from everywhere, lights flashed, lasers shot across the room, and then, suddenly, a spotlight beamed down on an overweight transvestite in a huge green gown with a bright red boa. He went into "The Lady Is a Tramp," and the whole crowd loved it. After a few jokes, the host announced that employees would not be the only ones on stage tonight and that they would also be having a "Best Amateur Drag Queen Contest." Layla had excused herself to the bathroom and was missing out on all of the fun. I filled her in when she came back, and she seemed even more excited than I had imagined. The show's intermission finally ended, and the Madam came back out to announce the volunteer contestants.

"First we have Diego Baltadano from Houston, Texas!" An overweight man got on stage waving his hands.

"Next up, all the way from London, please welcome Miles Stevenson!" An inebriated blond pale man in women's jeans got up and ripped off his shirt.

"Our last entry is a friend from right here in Manhattan! Please welcome the latecomer, Callum Littlefield!" Nobody got up. I was laughing and looking around the room for the next moron to show his face, when Layla leaned over and kissed me on the forehead.

"Gotcha!" she smiled, as two men in white thongs and roller skates grabbed my arms and escorted me to the stage. There was no way out.

Layla grinned from ear to ear. I was happy that she was enjoying herself so much and thought that I might as well play along. Even if it was at my expense. I didn't know anyone there, anyway. Who cared if I was making a fool of myself? I was going to win. The contest was made up of three events. One, best outfit. Two, best body. And three, best "booty shaker."

Best outfit was not really up to us, as we were each dressed by three personal tranny stylists. I could not tell what the other guys were wearing, but the show had me in a full-out Cleopatra gown and headdress. I was the last to go and wondered how Layla was going to react to this. I couldn't be lame and just go through the motions. I had to show some personality. I heard the song "I'm Too Sexy" in the main room, and before I knew it, I was pushed out on stage and told to do my thing. So boom. There I was, on stage in the East Village, in front of New York's trendy elite and the girl for whom I had fallen, scantily clad in the clothes of a glamorous Egyptian whore. I froze. But then I saw the audience clapping to the music and I locked eyes with Layla. She seemed to be hanging on for dear life upon my next move. So . . . I started to shake my hips. I went from stiff, to sort of bouncing my ass a little and shaking my hips to the music, to a full-out model's runway walk, capped off with me throwing my headdress into the audience and blowing a kiss to the panel of cross-dressed judges. I took that event by a landslide.

The next event was best body. Not much I could do with this one . . . all we had to do was take off our shirts and flex. Miles, clearly, already had a passion for this and gave various impressive poses. Diego was kind of a fat ass, but still much stronger than I. That left this skinny runt for last. I thought I at least had second in the bag, but I guess the judges were more impressed by bulk than definition. Oh well. That left me even with Miles, and the "booty shake" event left for the tiebreaker.

I knew that this one was mine. Those poor guys had no chance. They were drunk, but I was motivated. Layla had signed me up for this, so I had to win it for her. Miles came out and did his flex routine again, followed by some sort of humping jig. Diego actually wasn't too bad. He had a little Latin flavor and impressed the crowd with a salsa. It was sort of repetitive, though, and lacked flare. I had it. The DJ put on Michael Jackson's "Beat It," and I busted through the curtains with my best moonwalk. Once I reached the middle of the stage, I leg kicked out and swung through a three hundred and sixty degree spin. The crowd went wild, but my eyes never left Layla's smile.

"You were *SO GOOD!*" Layla exclaimed as I walked back to our table.

"Umm, yeah . . . that was not me. I swear."

"Looks like you've found your calling!" Layla gave me a big hug and we both sat back down.

"I'm going to kill you," I chuckled. "Seriously, you're dead."

"Aww. Why? So you can run off with your new love?" She motioned to one of the transvestite judges.

"Ladies, gentlemen . . . anything in between." The MC called for our attention again. "After much deliberation on our three beautiful contestants, the judges have decided that tonight's Best Amateur Drag Queen is none other than little Callum Littlefield!"

A man in roller skates approached me from behind and had me stand up to the applauding crowd. He wrapped a green boa around my neck and then placed a plastic crown on my head.

"Congratulations, honey." He lifted up my arms and blew his whistle.

"Will you be the bride or the groom?" Layla cackled when I got back to my seat.

"Very funny."

"I'm so proud!"

This semi-flirtatious, semi-sarcastic repartee went on for a while but quickly fizzled out once she began asking me about my family.

"Ehh, my fam is a tough one. Julia, my sister, is awesome. We're really tight and she's always looked out for me. I don't know . . . I guess my dad's pretty scary. He works a ton, he's competitive as hell, but he's a good guy. My mom's got her ups and downs too. She gets wrapped up in a lot of society bullshit, which drives me nuts, but that's her thing I guess. We don't see eye to eye much, but she cares. My grandmother is the true matriarch, though. You've *got* to meet her sometime." I told her about the Octopus, and her dresses, and the house, and my time trapped out on the Island.

"How *Grey Gardens*!" she laughed.

"Hah. Yeah, I guess. But it's pretty sad just sitting and watching her lose it. It makes me feel kind of helpless. I don't know. Let's hear more about you."

"Well, let's see. So I think I might really give the pre-med thing a shot. Art history will always be there and can be more of a hobby. And as for the teaching thing, it's the kids I love, so maybe I can be a psychiatrist at a school or something. Whatever, though. Plenty of time to change my mind and figure this all out. And you, young Littlefield? Penn . . . Finance . . . Yawn?"

"Well, the truth is, I'm not really satisfied with a few things right now. I mean not right 'right' now. I'm happy here. With you. But just in general, shit—every time I try to speak about myself it sounds like I'm bragging or complaining."

"I don't care, Callum. Just spit it out."

"No. It's nothing bad. My father assures me things should be . . ." Her eyes rolled back and I cut myself off. "What? What did I say?"

"I can't physically sit here and watch you morph into that stiff upper-crust forty-year-old-man mode again. Stop! You were in a dress on stage fifteen minutes ago! This isn't you."

I paused and thought about it.

"I guess it's weird. Okay, I don't have much to complain about." She leaned back and listened. "Life's not that fucked up at all. I got kicked out of Mather. Big deal. I'll still get into Penn. My parents are kind of assholes, but they care. So what? Isn't it that way for most teenagers? My friends hate me. Fuck them. Whatever. Layla—I'll stop. This is stupid."

"No, please, Cal. It's good." She grabbed my forearm and lightly pushed her thumb up and down my open wrist. Suddenly, I didn't feel so stupid. She was with me.

"I have everything else going for me. Life's financially comfortable, I'm healthy." I knocked on the wood table. "I'm getting a terrific education, and I probably have a great job waiting for me at the end of that tunnel. The future is pretty lucid and predictable. I have nothing to complain about."

"Sounds kind of boring to me," Layla replied. "Is that really what you want? A set script to life? I thought you were an author. What about writing your story? *Everyone* has a story, and you have the talent to get it out there."

"Well . . . it's not that simple."

"Cal, don't get me wrong. We're eighteen. We don't have to have answers, but you need to think about *options!*"

I thought about it. She was probably right. I looked at Layla and felt like I was looking at the world through a new set of eyes. There was more to me.

I told Layla more about the Octopus, and she loved it.

"I'm super close with my grandmother too," she said. "She's actually cool. She always tells me that I should have one date for drinks, one date for dinner, and one date for dancing *every* night."

"Wow. So how did it go before? And, more importantly, by when do I have to get you to your next appointment?"

"Shush. I think I'm killing three birds with one stone."

"Efficient."

"Something like that." And she smiled. "My grandmother also told me that I would never have problems finding a guy if I was always a little blonde and a little dumb. Isn't that ridiculous?"

"Well . . . I can kind of see where she is coming from." Layla slapped my hand across the table.

I went on about my summer and told her a bit about Miralva, but didn't want to weird her out. Layla was hooked on the subject, but I couldn't get too far into it. No. Not tonight.

"I totally understand if you don't want to talk about it, but it sounds like both of these women have had a serious impact on your life."

"No. Not really." I shut down the idea. "I'm really more of . . ." I let it go. "You know, I'm actually kind of bad at analyzing myself. My thoughts are really only clear when I write them down."

"Why don't you write more?"

"You asked me that already."

"It seemed appropriate to repeat."

"No, you're right. It just hasn't ever seemed like a reality."

It was such a simple question, yet more complicated than she could understand.

"I don't know. It's not a job really."

"Sure it is!"

I supposed that she was right, but it wasn't on my radar. My dad wouldn't have bought it.

"Well, I guess I have not really thought about it as anything serious."

"You should. Tell me some stories, Mr. Hemingway."

"No, it's not that. I mean I try to pretend sometimes, but I'm nothing legitimate or anything. I sort of just let my mind escape and whatnot. Writing lets me be anyone and do anything."

"Like . . . ?"

I went into a piece I wrote about Darnell Jones, Mather class of '77 and the first black student. It was totally fictional but based off of some guy I found in the yearbook and what I thought his life could have been like. Her eyes grew wider than I thought possible when I went into my stories, and she hung on to every word.

"Maybe I should just forget all this crap and pull a Thoreau. I like the idea of it. Running away and just writing. It's kind of mysterious or romantic, you know?"

"Well, I'd come with you." She smiled. I had never felt more comfortable. I know we had really just met weeks before, but at that moment I knew this was something special.

The restaurant was starting to clear, even though it felt like only a few minutes had passed.

"Thanks, Layla."

"Well . . ."

"Well what, Layla? Oh, you want to get out of here?" I was so aloof. "Sor—"

"Well aren't you going to kiss me, Cal?"

My heart skipped a beat, and I leaned over the table and kissed her briefly.

"About time, sir. Guess we should get back, though. Have to be up early for work tomorrow," Layla said, glancing at her watch.

I didn't want to leave. I was leaning in at that point and moved my hand across the table to hold on to hers. She tensed up for a second but then let me hold both of them.

Layla smiled and told me that she really should be going home, but I convinced her to stay for just a little longer. Before we knew it, Layla and I were the last ones in the restaurant. I wanted to hold her hand or put my arm around her as we walked back to the car but felt self-conscious. She thanked me over and over for dinner. We enjoyed most of the car ride uptown in a quiet peace. Even as we sat in this thick silent vacuum and I concentrated on the road, I could feel her looking at me. Her stare was hitting me in the triangle between my right cheek, ear, and eye. I kept smiling.

As we neared her building, Layla grabbed my hand and gave me a firm squeeze.

"You know how you were asking about Brooks from Princeton?" Her grip grew tighter and her fingers felt cold.

"Yeah?" I let out a nervous laugh. Layla began to tear up.

"What is it?"

"Nothing." Her breath was short. "He's just a creep and I really never ever want to talk about him. There was a stupid really horrible night months ago, way before I met you, but I want nothing to do with him. Ever." I pulled up in front of her building and turned the car off.

"Good," I said with a nervous smile.

We agreed to meet for lunch a few days later as she was going to Southampton with her parents. I got out to open the car door for her, but by the time I reached her, she was already out, leaning against the jeep, and looking at me with vast eyes under a wrinkled, almost mischievous brow. I took both of her hands, wished her goodnight, and kissed her as tenderly as I could. Her thin lips returned the kiss in a deep slow motion as her left hand went through my hair and caressed my earlobe. I pulled her away from the car, walked her to the door, and noticed that she was looking at the ground.

"Is something wrong?"

"No." She responded. "I just haven't kissed any—it's hard to explain. Don't worry, okay?"

I should have worried, but I was overwhelmed by the moment.

"I wish you could stay," she whispered, and she allowed her forehead to drop on my shoulder. I squeezed her body closer to mine, and she instinctively pulled back but then slowly allowed herself near me again.

"I'm not going anywhere, Layla. No rush."

32

MELON'S

I WAS DYING FOR MEAT. J.G. Melon's is my favorite lunch spot in the world and has the best burger in the City. Some argue for P.J. Clarke's farther midtown, but there's really no comparison. After three nights on the phone until two in the morning and three days of flirtatious text messages and emails, Layla and I planned to meet at Melon's for lunch that Sunday.

It was a breezy summer day and the Upper East Side was swinging in force. Mothers in pedal pushers and J. McLaughlin jackets strolled their babies toward the park. Boys in blue shorts marched around the corner toward the Buckley School summer program. Hungover college students in sandals, sunglasses, and polos bypassed the line of glaring eyes at Melon's toward their bacon-egg-and-cheeses at E.J.'s a block away. Overdressed women in their early thirties sat outside eating salads. Their melancholy, merlot eyes, framed with eye shadow and bronzer, scanned for potential husbands. Meanwhile, the princes for which they looked sat at the bar inside in the same Thomas Pink shirts, designer jeans, and loafers from the night before. They avoided the summer glare while wolfing down their Bloody Marys and recapping their debaucheries. These rakes were the kings of Melon's. Everyone was within two degrees of separation, and most were just one. Familiar faces and polite smiles were abundant.

I tried getting a table for two, but the rosy-cheeked Irish man told me that he could not seat me until my entire party had arrived. The place was packed and I knew we'd have to wait, but it was okay. It was a brisk summer day, and the food was worth the wait. Layla showed up with two huge bags from Bergdorf's and gave me a big kiss on the cheek.

"I had some time to do a little shopping before your distractions," she said with a guilty grin.

"Looks like you did well." We waited outside and I avoided eye contact with a few of my mother's friends. They were definitely talking about me. One of them, Mrs. Kinsley, had a son that was a sniffling, snot-nosed rat of a freshman at Mather and knew of my situation. The woman begged for eye contact, but I was a guard at Buckingham. Layla tapped me on the shoulder and pointed to three black guys on the corner singing to the customers sitting outside.

"The acapella bums! I love these guys," I told her. These three homeless men spent the warmer months on the Upper East Side making rounds outside of the restaurants lining Second and Third Avenues. They only knew two songs: "Sitting By The Dock of The Bay" and "What a Wonderful World." They were old and unthreatening and held warm smiles as they sang. My phone rang and I saw that it was Grandmaman, but I didn't interrupt the concert. They finished up their repertoire and Layla applauded as if she'd just seen The Rolling Stones.

I gave them a few bucks and we were soon called inside for our table. The fiery yet comforting host walked us to a table by the window in the back, which was unfortunately adjacent to a table with two guys I knew from growing up, Peter van Truesen and Henderson "Hendy" Balflow. They both had gone to St. Bernard's and rowed at Hotchkiss. They were the worst you could expect out of a bland, preppy upbringing. Pseudo cool kids. Both were complete losers growing up in the City. They sat around playing POGS or Dungeons and Dragons in their apartments, they didn't hang out with girls, and they had no visible athletic ability. With this combination, it was tough to be much of anything in middle school. They eventually went off to Hotchkiss and grew out of their awkward bodies and into Arian monsters perfect for rowing. The two realized that preppy was cool, that their families bled blue, and they soon considered themselves God's gift to the world. Not because they had any personality, not because they were original, not even because they were well liked, but simply because they learned how to fit in. I said hello, however reluctantly, and they both smiled and nodded.

This wouldn't be the end of our encounter. One of them was going to have to sneak in some kind of sarcastic remark. Middle school rivalries never died. I just sat there trying to count how many paintings of watermelons I could find on the wall before they thought of some genius thing to say.

"Looking gooood, CALOOM," said Balflow with a thick layer of cynicism. Fourteen. I wasn't going to bring myself down to his level. Not in front of Layla.

"Thanks, Hendy," and I turned my chair so that my back was facing them. I could tell from Layla's deliberate glance toward the menu that they were staring at her. I could hear them chuckle and whisper comments under their breath. It was getting obnoxious.

"Could you guys please cut it out? Grow up." I turned around to face them.

"What?!" Peter smiled and looked in my direction, but not actually into my eyes.

"Seriously?"

Hendy then sarcastically pushed his chair back a little and exclaimed, "ooooooooooooohhhhh."

I was ready to flip. Luckily the waitress arrived with their receipts and to take our orders.

"What assholes," Layla grimaced.

"Don't worry about them," I assured her. "They're complete tools."

"I know," she said. "You're better than that." I liked that she said that but wasn't entirely sure that it was true. I'd assume so for the time being.

We both ordered cheeseburgers and got a bowl of cottage fries to share. I also ordered a cup of chili with onions and cheddar to put on top of mine. Our juicy burgers came out soon, and we handled them with ease and ordered a slice of key lime pie for desert.

A fifty-something-year-old red-headed woman in khakis and a white polo shirt brought out the slice of pie, pulled a second fork from her apron, and placed it in front of me.

"Such a fine looking couple should share their treasures, you know," she said. Layla blushed.

"Well, you're welcome, Layla. Clearly, I raise our good-looks average," I joked.

"And who said we're to be considered a couple, Callum?"

As I fumbled for a witty response, Layla grabbed my hand and squeezed it. She then bent down and reached into her purse for a moment.

"Now I'm not trying to get rid of you by any means, Cal, but I saw this at our church and thought you might be interested for the rest of the summer."

"Hmmm?" I was skeptical.

To my dismay, Layla pulled the key lime pie away from me and passed a pamphlet across the table in its place.

The Palmetto Tree Retreat.

"Are you trying to send me to freaking *rehab*?!"

"Hah, no, dummy. Keep reading."

I opened the brochure to discover pictures of sandy beaches, open-air classrooms, a man on a porch with a notebook, and a woman behind a desk on a laptop.

"It's a writers' colony! I thought if you were really serious about all this, you might want to go down there for August before school or something."

She had actually thought of me.

"Layla . . . thanks. But I'm not that good. It would be a waste. This is for serious writers."

"We'll that's the point! To get serious. You'll get better. You'll get out what you put in, you know?"

"Yeah, but, you know I'm kind of in trouble, and I can't even imagine what my dad would think."

"Forget that, Cal! I know your dad loves you and wants the best, but think outside the box. You're eighteen!" She had a point. "Just at least *think* about it."

"Okay. I'll think about it."

And I would. I actually had trouble getting it off of my mind the rest of the meal. For once I felt like I might have a goal I could act upon. But I just didn't know how to go about it. My father would never agree. But who cared? I could do it on my own. People get jobs and work their way through school. That's what is done. Right? I had to get over it. Layla believed in me. I could do it.

"Hey, Layla, this is kind of from left field, but do you want to come out to Locust Valley tomorrow and meet the Octopus herself?" I wanted more time with Layla and I wanted to show her off. Plus Grandmaman would be so happy that I had come back; it might get me out of the doghouse. Besides, I thought the two ladies would like each other. "We could play tennis, swim in the Sound . . ." She made a face. "Oh, that's right. Excuuuse me. I should have known that girls who summer in Southampton don't swim in the Long Island Sound."

"Oh, shut up! I'll swim in it."

I rolled my eyes.

"Well it is kind of polluted, isn't it?"

"Haha. Wow. It's no Bathing Corp, but no pressure. Anyway, we could make a bonfire on the beach and roast marshmallows . . . whatever. It'll be fun."

"Yah, okay, great!

"And maybe you could spend the night at my place in the City tonight so we can head out there early . . . ?" It was worth a shot.

Layla tilted her head and gave me an embarrassed, yet confident smile. As if she knew I was up to something, but thought it was cute. She held her tongue for a solid five seconds and then giggled a little, put her face down so her hair gently tossed in front of her, and looked up.

"That would be nice, actually. I'll just tell my parents that I'm staying with one of my girlfriends for a few nights." I couldn't believe it. "I just need to run a few errands first. And logistically speaking, if you're planning to kidnap me for more than a day, I need to figure some things out."

"Important business at the nursery school?"

"Something like that."

I wished we could have stayed there for the entire afternoon, but I was so excited about that night and the next day that it didn't matter. She laughed because she could tell how excited I was. My phone kept vibrating, but I turned it off because nothing could be good enough to interrupt that moment.

"You know what, Layla?" I asked. "I'm going to show you that I'm more than a dejected offshoot of my dad. Even *I* am not that boring. I'm going to apply to that program. And I'm going to write you the great American novel. Something awesome." I felt like a child.

"Not for *me,* Cal! I don't think you're boring," she said. "You sometimes take yourself a little too seriously, but I really like the Callum I've been getting to know. Do it for him."

"Well, I like you too. A lot." I grabbed her fingers, and we both looked at the crumbs of our piecrust.

Layla hailed a cab shortly after, and I headed home to prepare for the night. This was going to be it.

33

RELEASE

A RED NUMBER FIVE blinked on a small, black box next to the kitchen phone. How could a simple prime number on an outdated little answering machine bring me back down to earth so quickly? Five messages. One angrier than the other. All from my father.

"You're out of bounds."

"After all we've done for you."

"A real embarrassment."

"On your own."

"Spoiled brat."

They all blended into one and other. I violently pressed erase after each message. My father rarely lost control of his temper. When he did, there was generally a legitimate reason, but this was a lack of communication. No. A lack of perspective.

I paced around the house. *This was the night. She was the one. Fuck you, Dad. Who do you think you are? Just apologize and comply. I don't want his life. Where is my mother when I need her? Forget them. I need condoms.*

I sat in the large brown leather chair behind my father's oversized oak desk and opened my laptop. I logged on to my email, looked at the brochure, and smiled. This was right.

Dear Dad,

I know that you are disappointed in me right now and that we have not been seeing eye to eye on just about anything, but I need you to try and understand me. I agree that I have been deliberately disobeying you and Mom this summer, and I'm sorry about the way I left Mather. I have not been doing anything morally wrong, though. We are on different pages right now and need to begin a real dialogue. I am a good kid and I'm just beginning to figure out what path I want to take. I need a change and I need it soon. Even if I'm readmitted, I will not be attending Penn in the fall. I know this kills you, but I am not ready for it. The only reason I was going there in the first place is because it was part of your master plan. I know you have done well and probably do know what's best for me, but I need to figure some things out for myself.

I'm going to enroll at the Palmetto Tree Retreat Writing Colony outside of Charleston, South Carolina, for the year. I have attached the website below. Maybe they will give me credits for school. I'm not sure. It's just something I need to do. I assume that you will not be financing this for me, and it does not matter. I'll get a job. Two jobs. Whatever it takes to pay for my classes, food, and lodging.

After that, I would like to revisit the topic of Penn again,
but right now it's not for me. Thank you for listening, and
I hope you understand.

Your son,
Callum

Send.

I did it. I don't know how, but it lifted a three-hundred-pound weight off of my chest. I could breathe. I could not wait for his response. But I would have to. I had bigger issues to attend to at the moment.

34

PREPARATIONS

I COULDN'T BELIEVE THAT this was finally happening. More so, I couldn't wait to tell Layla the news. I could see it now. She'd be proud. I was proud of myself. I would tell her over dinner, and we would return to my place and make love all over the house. I had to make everything perfect.

Layla said she had a bunch of errands to run and would arrive late. I wasn't much of a cook, so I made reservations at a couple of local restaurants. One was a cash-only local Italian spot, and the other was traditional American cuisine, but with a very Long Island/Nantucket feel to it. I also made sure to keep a couple of takeout menus handy, just in case she was too tired to go out. I sauntered down Madison to Patrick Murphy and bought Brie, pâté, and grapes for a snack. The food situation was under control. Next was booze. We had the good wine in the basement, guest wine in the fridge, a bottle of champagne, Mom's vodka, and my father's Scotch. That night was to be special, and Layla *was* a guest. I found the key to the wine cellar in my dad's medicine cabinet. I had known about this spot for years. Funny that his hiding the key to prevent me from drinking would eventually introduce me to his anxiety pills and painkillers. I headed down to the basement to select something impressive.

The basement was divided into four areas by white Asian drop screens. One was storage. Christmas ornaments, trunks for camp, luggage, old posters, toys, sports equipment, and really anything you could think of. The other area was a gym that probably hadn't been used more than five times since we moved in. It had a bicycle, a treadmill, and a few free-weights. Nothing notable, but enough for anyone with a spec of motivation.

The third area was my play space. This fifteen-by-fifteen area had gone through various transformations throughout my childhood. Over the years, it had seen hockey nets, a pool table, a boxing bag, a ping-pong table (later on used for quarters and flip cup), darts, athletic posters, movie posters, futons, bean bags, stereos, lava lamps, and leather chairs from my dad's old study. The room was in constant transformation. Its prime phase was probably in middle school when I used to have all of my friends and a bunch of girls over after school every Friday for spin-the-bottle parties. At that point I had a beaded door in the entrance, three lava lamps, shag carpeting, five been bags, and a futon. It was every middle school child's dream. We'd play everything from truth or dare to seven minutes in heaven (the wine cellar). One time someone accidentally knocked into and broke two five-hundred-dollar bottles of port. That was when Dad began to lock the room.

The wine cellar was one of Dad's hobbies. By no means was he a connoisseur, but he had expensive taste and ipso facto a strong collection of alcohol. I thought about bringing out a bottle of champagne but remembered the Boathouse and realized it *was* a little over the top. It symbolized celebration, and as much as I wanted to celebrate Layla, I didn't want to come off as a freak either. I decided to go with a Nuit St. Georges Burgundy from '99. I didn't know anything about it, other than the fact that it was on the top shelf and I knew Dad kept his best and most expensive wine up and out of reach. I also liked the picture on the label. It looked like a really cool mansion. I brought the wine up to the kitchen.

It was about six o'clock and the house was clean. Food and beverages were in check. I pulled out my phone and realized it had been off since Melon's. Six missed calls from Grandmaman. No. Not tonight. I texted Layla.

"Can't wait to see you!"

My phone buzzed soon after.

"You too! Might be 15 min late."

"No worries. See you soon."

I still needed condoms. I walked down the block to the Korean market. The Koreans behind the counter had known me since I was six and recognized me immediately. It used to be awkward when I went from buying candy to buying beer, but this felt even less comfortable. I looked at a pack of Trojans that said "shared sensation" and bought five packets just in case.

I was on my way back upstairs when I thought about potentially using my parents' room. They were gone and would never know. Besides, they had the biggest bed and an awesome bathroom with a marble bathtub. Just in case. Weird. No. Fuck it. Way too weird. Bringing Layla to my parents' room would freak her out. I went up to my room and put the condoms in my bedside table drawer.

It was already seven o'clock, and Layla said she'd come over at eight. Time to get ready. I hopped in the shower, masturbated to build endurance, shampooed and conditioned my hair, soaped up my body, and washed my face. I got out and noticed that I looked kind of puny in the mirror so I pumped out thirty pushups. Much better. I then rolled on an excessive amount of deodorant and brushed my teeth. My crisply ironed khakis felt warm against my legs, and I went back to my Dad's closet to borrow a pink checked Turnbull & Asser shirt. The shirt was too big, so I rolled up the sleeves. Casual. Perfect. I went down into the study, put a Gypsy Kings CD in the stereo, and watched the clock.

Eight thirty rolled around with no word from Layla. Maybe she had hit some traffic. Eight forty-five, still nothing. I called her cell phone but it was off. Maybe she was on the line with somebody else? Or no, she was probably trying to call me. I waited about a minute. No call. I tried again. Still no rings and right to voicemail. It was definitely off. Where the fuck was she? I called her house at nine and the line was busy. That was kind of annoying. I tried again five minutes later and it was still busy. Was this some kind of joke? Was she on the phone gossiping with her friends and losing track of time? I tried again and the line was still tied up. Fuck. I could not call anymore. She had caller ID. I didn't want her parents to think I was some kind of stalker or anything.

Still, she should have at least called me to tell me she was going to be late.

"Hey, Layla. It's me, Callum. Umm, just wondering what's up? Hope you'll be here soon. Can't wait to see you." What a stupid message. I didn't sound cool. All I could do was wait, and each moment felt like eternity. This sucked. I was losing time like I lose cufflinks. I tried watching TV but could not pay attention. Around ten thirty I subliminally lost hope and cracked open the bottle of wine. I thought I should at least try and enjoy this. What bullshit. I sat by the window and watched cars drive by. My head perked up every time a cab pulled up, but it was never her.

I needed a change of scenery around eleven, so I moved downstairs to the kitchen. My phone had better reception in there, and I could still look at the cabs outside the window. By 11:10 I was pretty distraught. The night was hopeless. Dream crushed.

I finally checked my grandmother's messages. Standard, "Callum, are you coming out tomorrow?"; "Callum, it's your Grandmaman. Please call me back"; and then to my horror, "Callum, I need your help. Please come out here. It's Miralva. She is acting queer again."

Layla still might come, but Grandmaman needed my help. I had to be there for the Octopus. No matter what. This was on me.

I called Layla. The line went straight to voicemail again and I left another message.

"Hey, Layla, not sure what happened to our plans and all, but it turns out that I really have to run to Long Island. We're having a minor emergency concerning . . . and, well . . . whatever. I'll explain it to you later. Not sure what's going on, but I hope you're not already on your way over here. Call you later."

35

FACING MIRALVA

THE HIGHWAY WAS EMPTY and I felt tipsy. I blasted the air conditioning to stay awake and made it to Locust Valley in record time. I parked the car and noticed there was hardly any moonlight. We usually got very starry evenings at that point in the summer. The night was pitch-black and the air was thick and sweet. All of the house lights were off and I stumbled on the gravel toward the front door. Crickets chirped in the distance and the pebbles crunched beneath my loafers. I've always found the country more unsettling than the City, and the eerie quiet sent chills down my spine. I walked into the house and nothing looked very different. The dark Cuzco School painting of the Virgin Mary still hung in the entranceway under a weak bulb. Oil shimmered back. The portrait of my grandparents still sat above the first-floor landing. The chandeliers still glimmered reflections off any suggestion of light. The floor was still warped and slanted. Everything was fine. Just excruciatingly quiet. I wished someone would turn on the television.

I went to my grandmother's room and found her door locked. I knocked, murmuring that it was just me.

"Are you alone, baby?"

Her voice was higher and more feeble than ever. I assured her that I was. She opened the door for me covered in pearls and a gold satin nightgown. *THUMP—SMASH*. She dropped her drink. The glass made a loud crash on the floor, and I heard a moan that led into a scream from upstairs. My grandmother covered her ears. Cranberry juice dripped down her dress and soaked into the carpet. Grandmaman was pale and short of breath. I had never seen her so scared. I tucked her into bed and noticed an open Bible on her nightstand and worn-out rosary beads hanging from her reading lamp.

"Oh, Mosquito. I am so glad you are here. She has been at it again. I think she has put curses on this house. Something is wrong. I have heard her screaming and singing all day, and she has not come out of the attic since yesterday morning. I can't climb up there. I'm too old and the rest of the 'slaves' are terrified. They are all very religious, you know. Where have you been?"

"I'm here now. Why didn't you call the police?" I asked.

"I don't want those people in my house, Mosquito. They'll take everyone away. Besides, she hasn't done anything wrong."

"Should we call a priest?" I asked.

Grandmaman looked at me like I was helpless. No country club minister could handle something like this. An exorcism was a long way from a Piping Rock wedding. This was in my hands.

I told her to stay near the phone and listen in case I called out. By now my legs were trembling so hard I was afraid my knees would give out. I called out Miralva's name a few times as I climbed up the old attic steps to warn her that I was coming. The narrow staircase was uncarpeted, and the wood creaked under each step. I felt a crunch beneath my foot and saw that Miralva had thrown a mirror down the corridor. There were thin shards of glass everywhere, and the frame sat in two pieces a few steps above. The passage was dark and I swung my arms in hopes of finding the hanging chain to illuminate the single bulb screwed above the steps. I found the cord and pulled. Click. The light made a soft comforting buzz, and I carried forward. I looked to the base of her door and saw a pair of reading glasses perched over an open Bible lying in front of the door. Thoroughly underlined. Obsessively underlined. Notes and drawings in margins. "Ogum" and "Xango" written repeatedly on several pages. The Macumba deities were back. Four knives surrounded the book in the formation of two crosses. I took two more steps.

"Stopy, stopy!" Miralva called back in broken English. "Everything fine. He watch and save." Her English had improved. "*Vai embora!*" But I heard the door unlock from the inside. I paused for it to open, but nothing. I knocked on the door. No response. I knocked again, and I heard a whimper for me to go away. I put my hand on the door.

"LEAVE ME ALONE! I DON'T NEED YOU!" she screamed.

I took a deep breath and opened the door to find Miralva on the floor in the back of the room surrounded by pink candles. The room smelled like cherry Starbursts. I could hardly breathe. A Brazilian picture book of saints and prayers had been torn apart and thrown across the room. Underlined pages and pictures were pinned on the walls above her twin bed.

Miralva was curled over in a fetal position weeping uncontrollably at the base of some sort of shrine. A small ottoman from the living room sat in front of her, covered in red monogrammed towels from the pool house and black dishtowels she must have found on her own. She had placed one of my grandfather's wood cufflink boxes on the ottoman and filled it with rice. As I inched closer, I noticed the smell of eggs but saw no trace of them. One of my sister's old Baby Troll dolls was also in the box. The doll was cradling a half-smoked Philly's Blunt cigar and had three shot glasses surrounding the base of its little troll feet: one filled with whiskey, one with rum, and one with red wine. Miralva lay at the base of the offering weeping and humming an unidentified slow tune, avoiding eye contact with the shrine and with me.

I warily stepped into the scented Macumba chapel and sat down next to her. No response. I touched her shoulder and found her body freezing cold in a deep sweat. She batted my hand away and curled up again, this time moving around more and whimpering with pain. I crawled around her and saw her violently tearing at her left forearm, scratching from wrist to elbow. Up-down, up-down.

"Stop it right now, Mi! It's just me, Callum. *Para agora!*"

I immediately grabbed her arms and spoke with a surprisingly firm tone.

Her arms were raw to the flesh. She hadn't hit an artery but was bleeding bad. She looked at me with a blank stare and then went right back for her wrist, as if she could sneak by me, this time gnawing with her teeth.

"No! STOP it, Miralva!" and I moved behind her to trap her arms with a bear hug. She screamed, struggled, kicked, and then collapsed into a deep cry, letting her neck and head fall back over my shoulder.

"It's okay, Mi. It's just me, Callum. Your friend."

She cried more, leaned over, slapped the wall leaving a bloody trace, and began to sob into the carpeted floor. She was exhausted and could not control her pulsing lungs enough to respond. I thought about calling the police. But my grandmother would not want it, and it would be probably the worst thing I could do to Miralva. I sat there trying to bandage her wounds, holding a blanket around her and telling her that things would be okay. Like a toddler after a temper tantrum she had difficulty breathing. No words, just soft whimpers and heavy gasps. I wondered where this all came from. How had she broken down again? There was a bulletin board above her bed covered in Christmas card pictures of Julia and me. I felt like shit. We called her crazy because she made shrines and lit candles, but who was to say we were not crazy for praying on our knees and taking wheat wafers to feel closer to God? Did our rejection drive her insane?

Miralva calmed down over the next few hours. I told her that I was going to have to take her to the hospital to take care of her arm. She looked scared, but she knew it was coming. No complaints. She didn't say another word. I drove her to Glen Cove Hospital, explained everything to the doctors in the emergency room, and returned to the Octopus.

I got home to find Grandmaman asleep on her chaise lounge in front of the weather channel. She didn't seem to know where she was when I woke her, and I led her back into bed as I had countless times before.

That night I fell asleep in Grandmaman's bed holding her hand. Maybe to make her feel better, maybe because I was terrified, maybe a little bit of both.

36

BROKEN FLOWERS

MY PHONE, VIOLENTLY vibrating against my leg, startled me awake. The Octopus lay next to me asleep. I looked at the bedside clock: 11:00 AM. Last night. Miralva. Layla still hadn't called. This might be her. I didn't want to disturb Grandmaman, so I snuck off to the other room. It was Patterson. Fuck. This was the last thing I needed. I reached to the phone to press the ignore button just as I realized that he might be with Layla.

"Collin, this better be fucking good," I said with a stern voice. I expected blaring music and deafening shrills from drunken girls in the background, but his end was silent.

"It's not, man," Patterson said in a solemn voice. "Layla got into a horrible car accident yesterday." Complete silence. "She didn't make it."

"You're kidding, right?" I knew he wasn't joking. "This is a horrible fucking joke. You're a sick fuck to be calling me like this. Do you know the kind of shit I have been through the last few hours?"

"I'm sorry, man. It's not. I don't know any of the details, but Layla passed away, bro. I'm so sorry."

"I, ugh, I gotta go. Thanks for calling."

Layla couldn't be dead. We had lunch yesterday. She was fine. She was young, happy, and beautiful. I was going to be a writer now. Miralva went nuts. The Octopus needed me. What the fuck was Patterson talking about? This had to be some kind of dream. I pinched myself and checked my phone compulsively. Yeah, I had really just talked to Patterson. I smashed my phone against the wall.

"FUUUUUUUCKKKKKK!" I yelled.

Grandmaman called groggily from bed.

"One sec," I yelled back.

This could not be happening. Not to Layla. Why her? She was perfect. She hadn't done anything wrong. Why wasn't I crying?

What could I do? I needed to leave. I wanted to be alone. I went back into my grandmother's room and squatted by her side.

"Grandmaman, I'm sorry to leave, but my friend, the one I mentioned, she died last night." She was confused, but so was I, and I had nothing else to say. She squeezed my hand twice. I kissed her on the forehead, left her a note reiterating my excuse for leaving, and walked out the door.

When I got back to the City, I didn't know what to do. I had nowhere to go. I lay on my bed and stared at the ceiling, my mind racing. Miralva was as good as gone, Grandmaman was dying, and Layla was dead. I fell asleep fully clothed and above the covers, finally coming to around ten. It was like I was watching myself as I walked downstairs to the bar, poured half a glass of vodka, and took it down in one gulp. I gagged, threw up a little in my mouth, and swallowed it down again. I drank two quick glasses of wine from the back refrigerator. I felt nothing. I tried throwing water on my face, even putting my head under the faucet. It felt forced. Numb.

I walked outside to find the streets totally empty. Park Avenue was deserted. I walked by one couple and overheard the woman say, "Oh, please. I only go to the *West* Side when I'm taking the boat to Europe."

The man laughed as if it was the funniest fucking thing he had ever heard. I wanted to turn around and tackle him. Tackle them both to the ground and punch them and tear their eyes out. Pound their heads into the pavement. Where the fuck *was* everybody? I walked down the middle of the street just waiting for a car to come. Maybe a truck or a bus. None did.

The City was hot, steaming, my shirt was sticking to my lower back, and my crotch itched. The MetLife building was getting closer, and I decided to stop. I sat down on the curb of the island between 54th and 55th Streets and started digging out marigolds. I wanted to destroy something. I pulled from the roots like the Octopus had taught me. I had dirt up my nails and made a mess: dirt and broken flowers everywhere. Though the air was humid and warm, the stone curb was cold and I felt a chill through my khakis. I took a break and was about to get back into the dirt when I noticed a skinny, shivering crackhead in ripped warm-up pants and a piss-stained T-shirt walking toward me from across the street.

I stood up and glared at him.

"BACK THE FUCK OFF!" I screamed, and I pitched a fistful of dirt and flowers in his direction. I then turned around and walked uptown. He was going to kill me. Definitely going to stab my neck with a hypodermic needle. Why couldn't God have taken someone like him instead of someone as pure as my Layla?

I reached 89th Street and made my way toward the Church of Saint Thomas Moore. I woke up a few homeless men on my way inside, but neither party really cared. I sat down at the second pew. Jesus was staring at me. Mary was staring at me. Various angels looked down at me. There was no point in all this bullshit. All these decorations. All the ceremonies and formalities. I asked God why on earth would he take Layla away. No response. Everything good in my life was gone. I'd do *anything* if he could bring her back. Still nothing. He just stared. Everybody stared.

37

THE NEXT DAY

I WOKE UP THE NEXT morning confused if it had all been a dream or not. I prayed that it had been. I felt weird. Removed from everything. I picked up my cell phone with the cracked screen and checked my calls. Fuck. Just as I had feared. Outgoing: Layla, Layla, Layla, Layla. Incoming: Grandmaman, Patterson.

No dream. She was dead.

Patterson forwarded me an email sent from her best friend, Catherine. "I'm so sorry, bro," he wrote above the body of the letter. The Semmerings had given her the details of the tragedy and told her to disseminate the information amongst her friends. Layla had died just after 6:00 PM on July 26. She was driving back from New Cannaan and had lost control of her mother's car and veered lanes, only to be hit by a larger SUV. Her car flipped two times into a large maple tree on the side of the Merritt Parkway. The accident broke her left arm and three ribs and left her in a coma. Layla remained in her coma for four hours before slipping away. There was too much internal bleeding for the doctors to do anything.

My face was a cold stone wall as I thought about where I was when she had crashed. Six o'clock. I had just texted her. Was she writing me back while she was driving? Where was I when she was fighting for her life? Where was I when she passed? I was buying fucking pâté and condoms. I was mad at her for being late. I was a prick. Everything in Long Island happened after she was already dead. I thought of her face, her enormous eyes, her chuckle, and her encouragement. And then I could not think anymore.

What else was there? I barely knew her. I would have done about anything for her, yes. But I was making this too much about me. I was only eighteen years old. What the fuck was I doing? It's not like we were married or anything. What about her other friends? What about her *family*? I wanted to order flowers. I needed to be a part of this. Our worlds were just coming together. Things were about to be right. Now I was alone.

38

THE FUNERAL

AS I CLIMBED UP THE STEPS of the Southampton church, a middle-aged couple threw me a disapproving look as they walked past me. I got an awful feeling that I didn't belong. I checked myself out in the reflection of the glass covering the service schedule and deemed that my presence was appropriate. The church was large. Too big for this kind of service. Sure it was almost full, yeah, but that was only because the entire Groton student body in addition to its most recent graduates were in the audience in their own roped-off section. They were behind the family section. I had no section. I was random. It should not have been that big. It should have been more personal. The family, a minister, and me. I took a seat in the last pew on the left and scanned the crowd. Lots of kids. Some of them never even overlapped with Layla. They probably had no idea who she was. It didn't feel like a funeral. Girls were fixing their hair, guys were roughhousing and then looking down with smirks on their faces when hushed. It felt like a school meeting or a lecture at Mather.

A tingle of nervous excitement pulsed through the crowd, like this was an event. Something different to get people out of their daily rhythms.

I recognized some faces in the crowd, but most were strangers. I felt like an uninvited guest. I could see the Semmerings in the front. Mrs. Semmering was half hostess, half heartbroken mother. She wore a black cocktail dress and lipstick and had donned a dark veil over her face. I spotted her turning her head around various times checking on who was there to bid farewell to her daughter. She'd make eye contact and mouth "thank you" to several of them. Yes, I could also see the pain in her face, but it didn't seem like enough pain. More just age. Mr. Semmering, on the other hand, looked like a stoic self-made businessman who had just witnessed his life's work go bankrupt. He sat up straight and stared forward as his wife held his lifeless arm. His face was pale and empty, the muscles around his mouth sagged tiredly, and one of his eyelids hung much lower than the other. This man was engulfed by death's fatigue. I had to strain my neck to catch a glimpse of what must have been Layla's two older siblings and her grandparents, but could not see much more than the back of their necks.

I thought about my own funeral. Who would come to mine? I had always thought I would die young. My mom would make a great show of it. She would put on a better show than Mrs. Semmering. She's more dramatic. I had no idea how my dad would act. I like to think he'd take it pretty hard. He had some serious goals for me. They'd be sad, of course. Would my friends from Mather come? Probably not. It was hard to believe we'd once been basically brothers. Not even that long ago. I missed that camaraderie. Maybe they'd come and feel horrible about the way they treated me. They'd realize that the list wasn't my fault and that it could have happened to anyone. They would appreciate my friendship and all of the great times we had and wish that I were still around. I wondered if any girls would show up. But then again, why would they?

As the minister approached the altar, I heard a muffled cackle from a shaggy red-headed boy two rows in front of me and saw another kid give him a quick dead-arm punch to shut him up. This reminded me of my grandfather's funeral when all of the kids went outside to play Red Light Green Light after the service. But come on. We were *seven*! I hoped that people would somber up quickly.

I thought about Grandmaman and how she should have the biggest funeral of them all. An international society ball. No, she didn't keep in touch with anyone anymore. All her friends were probably dead. She'd probably just be cremated and sprinkled over her vegetable garden. I'll have the beet salad with a sprinkle of grandmother, please. Gross. Perhaps buried with her pets. Her descent came so quickly. She really had needed me this summer.

The minister mentioned how Layla used to work at the church's day camp every summer and that she singlehandedly organized the arts and crafts fair. He said that Layla's smile could illuminate a room and that the kids would always cry in the parking lot because they would rather stay with her than go home to their parents. A boy once asked his father if Layla could come live with them. I smiled. Mrs. Semmering gasped loudly and burst into tears when the minister acknowledged the Semmerings' bravery. He said that the hardest and most unnatural thing in life was to bury one's child. Her cry sounded like Miralva's. Mrs. Semmering's elevated level of sorrow made me feel a little bit better. There we go. Let it out. The minister was an eloquent man and made me feel a little happy when he said that God takes away the world's best for his own company. I knew it was kind of cliché, but it made sense. Kind of. And I liked it. I thought that Grandmaman would go soon as well. It made me feel lucky to have known her. Both of them.

The next person to speak was Layla's friend Catherine. Catherine was the one who had sent the email. I did not know her, but she seemed nice and generally cute. I wonder if Layla had even mentioned me. Most of her eulogy focused on telling a story about another girl's death in a drunk-driving accident and how Layla was the glue that held everyone's world together after that. She was bawling throughout her words and had to stop on several occasions to compose herself. This was true sadness, true enough to finally help me release a few tears of my own. She finished by saying how much she missed her two friends and hoped that they were getting a manicure and going shopping together up in heaven. The levy was breaking. I could taste the warm salty drip over the right side of my mouth.

The next guy to speak was a male cousin no older than twenty-five. One cliché after another. I didn't know if I should be amused or angry.

"You're in a better place,"

"You were always everyone's favorite,"

"You were and ARE the wind beneath our wings,"

"Only the good die young,"

Thank God he was brief and the outgoing procession soon followed.

The wood coffin must have been some sort of heavy oak. I could see the strain on the faces of the pallbearers as they walked up the aisle carrying Layla away from me forever. I noticed a vein visibly pulsing up one portly man's neck. I couldn't believe she was actually in that box. I wanted one more chance to say good-bye. They carried her outside and into the hearse as everyone else followed and convened outside of the building. I don't know why, but seeing all these handsome well-dressed people on a beautiful day outside of a Church in Southampton really made me think of Miralva and how different her life was. She must have thought she was on another planet. Who were we to push her into this? I'd have gone nuts too.

I was the last person out of the church, and as I stood at the top of the steps and glanced over the crowd mingling on the lawn, I lost my sense of purpose. I didn't want to join. I felt betrayed. It was a cocktail party, or a reunion. People were hugging each other and laughing. I went back inside and sat back down in my pew.

I wasn't alone, though. There was a big guy with shaggy blond hair down in front bawling. I could see his shoulders shake as he buried his face in his hands. At least someone else there felt as bad I as I did. I automatically liked him. He was in my boat. I wanted to give him a pat on the back and grab a few beers so we could go talk about how miserable we were without Layla. We were brothers, and I wondered who he was.

I didn't know what to do in there. I didn't want to deal with the party outside, but I also didn't want to leave yet. It was too soon. I wasn't ready to go, so I sat in my pew taking in the architecture and decorations of the church. Then I felt bad for not thinking about Layla, so I did. I thought about her face, her smile, our dance, our dinner, our boat ride, my plans for the future, my plans for that night. I stopped. I surrounded three Our

Fathers with two Hail Marys because it made me feel better. I was afraid to move forward, but I knew I couldn't stay stuck in one place.

I walked out of the large stone building and saw the guy from the front row get into a Land Cruiser with Hotchkiss and Princeton Lacrosse stickers on it. Brooks? It had to be. I thought about the rumors Patterson had passed to me. How he was known to be "aggressive" with girls and about Layla's reaction to his name alone. Why was he so mortified? What had he done to her? His Land Cruiser pulled away and left a sense of comfort within me, as I knew that we were different. Layla knew she could trust me.

Great. Now I was alone. Patterson was talking to Mr. Semmering under a big willow tree by the parking lot. Maybe I'd join them. Then I thought about my brief connection with his daughter and felt out of place again. He probably had never even heard my name before. He'd shake my hand and be courteous, but the connection would end there. But maybe he'd understand. I'd say, "Sir, I'm sorry for your loss. I was in love with your daughter and had planned on marrying her." He would give me a stern yet respectful look and shake my hand like I was a man. We would be in the same club, the guys who really cared. Forget everyone else and their receptions. Mr. Semmering and I would find a dark pub and drown our sorrows away.

I snapped out of my daze when I noticed Patterson pointing at me and then Mr. Semmering walking toward me with a blank face. I looked down and pretended to be lost in thought.

"Are you Callum?" I braced myself.

"Yes sir." I responded. "Callum Littlefield." I shook his cold stiff hand. "I'm so sorry about Layla." Nothing better came out, but I *was* sorry about Layla.

"Well, we all are. It is a very difficult time, but we appreci-ate your support." He was not much better. I felt relieved. No punches yet. "I have something for you." Oh no, I thought. He's going to say a "knuckle sandwich" or a "beat down." No, he would not have said that. He would just deck me in the eye or nose and lay me out cold. The eye would be better. Broken nose sounds painful. He'd watch me fall and walk away.

"We found this in the car after the accident, and it appears to be a gift from Layla to you. She had been on her way back from picking it up in Connecticut." He handed me a leather-bound notebook.

"I don't know what to say. Thank you very much, sir."

"Well, she loved giving gifts. I think she's watching us right now. Watching people open her presents was probably her most favorite thing in the world. Take care of yourself." He walked away and back toward his wife and the minister, and just like that, I stood there dumbfounded. Mrs. Semmering looked at me and smiled.

It was beautiful. My name was inscribed in the front cover, and the inside flap had another inscription saying, "Keep Writ-ing! Love, Layla." I brought it up to my face and smelled the leather. "Thank you," I whispered into the notebook.

I cried the entire drive home. Things were starting to make sense.

39

THE INEVITABLE

MY PARENTS CAME HOME three days after the service and threw a fit. They saw the depleted liquor cabinet. They realized that my writing class only met twice a week and assumed I hardly went. They said that I had behaved horribly toward my grandmother, and they acknowledged my complete lack of respect for them and their trust. I only hoped that the Octopus had stood up for me a bit.

My father called me into his office the following night, sat me down across from him, and passed me a letter from the University of Pennsylvania's admissions office.

We are pleased to inform you that we stand by our decision and welcome you to the class of 2006 . . . I was still in. Before I could say a word, he passed me a check for ten thousand dollars.

"This should cover you for one semester at the Palmetto Tree Retreat, Callum. After that, you are on your own until you decide to get your life started again in Philadelphia."

Shocked and happy, I was ready to start living.

"Thank you, Dad."

I'd go back to Locust Valley for the rest of the summer and take care of Grandmaman. The Octopus needed me. We'd be good together. I'd keep her spirits up, and maybe she could whip me into shape. I figured Miralva would be hospitalized for a while or sent back to Brazil, but if not, I wouldn't mind living with her. I could help her. My parents could only yell, which would make me resent them more. The Octopus gave me work. Work kept me busy and took my mind off of things. This would be good for me.

My mother entered the room, kissed the top of my head, and joined my father behind the desk. My very own "American Gothic." They had another idea.

"I just spoke to your grandmother," my mother informed me. "Perhaps we have been a little too hard on you. It sounds like you have had a very difficult past few days, and we want to make sure you're all right. I can't believe we put you in that position with Miralva again, sweetie. I am so sorry."

My father gently took the drink out of my mother's hand and placed in on the other side of the desk. Mom looked down and placed her hand on his shoulder. "Grandmaman said she has never seen you act so brave." She began to tear. "I'm also so sorry about your friend, Callum. What was her name?"

"Layla. I'm fine, thanks. I just think I should get out of the City and back to Grandmaman's before South Carolina. She really needs me out there."

My parents glanced at each other.

"And Miralva, Callum, are you sure that you're okay? I would just feel so much more comfortable if you saw a doctor. Counseling can be so—"

"I'm fine, Mom. I promise. Please."

My dad looked at me with approval but gave me other unexpected news.

"Son, you're not going back to Locust Valley. We probably should not have put you in that situation in the first place."

They knew that Grandmaman did not really have control of me or of herself for that matter. I guess it was ridiculous to think that I could get away with spending the rest of the summer on the island.

"What you need is a fresh start," my father continued. "A controlled atmosphere, away from all of this nonsense. Something that will give you a chance to put things in perspective and learn how to work with your hands."

"Okay, but where—"

"South Dakota."

"Is this rehab? Dad, I'm not—"

"It's not rehab, Callum. It's just a program to get you out of your comfort zone for a bit, to give you a chance to think things over. Besides, Callum, things in Locust Valley are about to go through some changes . . . all for the better, of course, but it would not suit you to be there."

What do you mean?"

"Well, Miralva is going to remain in the hospital for a few more weeks and then be sent back to Brazil to an assisted living psychiatric center. She is sick, son, and we're going to help her. Also, your grandmother is going to move to a nursing home. The family has decided to put the house up for sale."

I was in disbelief. The world as I knew it was crumbling.

"I assure you that she will be very happy and comfortable. It just does not make sense anymore, Callum. Both in terms of her health and the family's finances." My father reached for my mother's trembling hand. I was afraid she was going to burst. I was afraid we were all going to burst.

40

NEXT

MY EYELIDS FEEL LIKE they're fighting lead weights. I haven't slept in a week and have officially slammed into the wall. I fight them off. He is looking at me. He wants to talk to me. My head nods off up and down, and while I want music, I'm too tired to ask. Besides, Dad would hate it. I lean my head against the jack hammering car window and watch the world bounce around. I sneak a glance and see my dad, with his coat over his suspenders, drafting some sort of motivational good-bye speech in his head. I knew he'd do this before I left. His eyes are set straight ahead. His lips are moving inaudibly. This must be awkward for him, as I imagine he doesn't know where to start. *I* don't even know where to start.

It's August and he still has his coat on. Shirt buttoned all the way, with his tie tied tight. After a long period of time, he clears his throat.

"Callum . . ."

He knows I'm fake asleep. "Yeah," I answer.

"Sit up straight. This trip is going to make or break you. Important time in your life. Hope you know this."

I rub my eyes and look out the window.

"Are you listening?"

"Yeah—I mean yes. Of course I know this is big."

"Sure. Well, Callum, I realize times have been tough for us recently. Especially for you. But I refuse to let you use that as an excuse for your behavior the past few months. You know that this might be one of your last chances to get back on the right foot. Penn can still very well take back their acceptance letter. We are lucky that they haven't done so. You have to put on your best behavior out there. This will not be like our last trip out West, Callum. It is not a resort ranch. These guys are going to be tough, and they don't want to hear one complaint. Especially from a kid like you."

"Thanks." Always knows how to get me motivated.

"I mean it. These guys are going to be real cowboys, and they are going to whip you into shape. I just want to warn you and let you know that it will be worth it in the end. This is going to give you a chance to do a lot of thinking and put your head back on your shoulders. Do you understand what I'm saying, Cal? This might be your last chance."

"Yes sir. Got it." And I really do have it. I'm ready to extricate myself from my childhood and grow up. The Towne Car pulls up to the curb. I walk to the rear of the vehicle, and my dad helps me take my luggage out of the trunk.

"Well. This is it." I shake his hand.

"I'm proud of how you're handling this, son. I'm sorry about the past few months." He pulls me in and wraps his other arm around me. "You know we're just trying help you, right, Cal? I love you. Your mother and I love you so much."

And all crap aside, deep down I know it's true. I bury my head into his shoulder and squeeze him.

"I know, Dad. I love you too. I just need to figure out how to do things on my own."

"I know you will."

I walk through the revolving glass door and see that the day's only flight to Pierre is on time. Here we go.

Next stop, South Dakota. I am going to be a ranch hand for the rest of the summer. I don't know what that means, exactly, but I assume it involves waking up early, milking cows, and building fences for the rest of the day. This particular ranch has a program for the young and privileged that have steered off the beaten path. I'll be there for seven weeks and then spend one week on an intensive outdoor spiritual leadership hike. Normally, I would flip. No fucking chance. And I'd fight it. I'd go to my mother, who would sympathize with me. To her, this sounds more like hell than anything she could imagine. I'd get them against each other and into loud horrible fights until they become fed up and quit. It wouldn't be difficult, but it doesn't seem worth it. I want to go.

Long Island Augusts, Labor Day dances, back-to-school parties, fall weekends in the City. Nothing is going anywhere. I don't need to keep up. I look back through the revolving door and see my father's car pull away. Thoughts of the Octopus, Miralva, and Layla churn through my mind. Though a sadness lingers, I hold their memories in my heart and, for the first time, push forward toward independence.

Thank you to:

3637

Zeke Hansen, my cousin, for the original version's cover art. You captured the Octopus better than I could have possibly hoped.

My late great aunt, Margot, for *Remembrance of Things Past.*

Alex Hoyt, my advisor and coach, thank you for believing in me from the first draft.

To Sophie Newbold, for the million favors and requests along the way. Thank you for capturing the story in such a vivid and memorable image.

To the team at Counterpoint and Softskull Press, thank you for your faith, patience, and hand holding along the way. Liz, Kelly, Nicole, and Julia—thank you for making this happen.

Dad and Carolina, thank you for your coaching, encouragement, and support. BFIE.

Many many many thanks to my mother, Mercedes Dorson, who has cheered my creative side from the beginning. Although she did not approve of various parts of this book (as most parents would not), she has been a dedicated editor, encouraging friend, and loving mother throughout the whole process. I could not have done it without you, Mom. Thank you.